The Lydia Chronicles

The Lydia Chronicles

Doris Read

A DUTTON BOOK

DUTTON
Published by the Penguin Group
Penguin Books USA Inc., 375 Hudson Street,
New York, New York 10014, U.S.A.
Penguin Books Ltd, 27 Wrights Lane,
London W8 5TZ, England
Penguin Books Australia Ltd, Ringwood,
Victoria, Australia
Penguin Books Canada Ltd, 2801 John Street,
Markham, Ontario, Canada L3R 1B4
Penguin Books (N.Z.) Ltd, 182–190 Wairau Road,
Auckland 10, New Zealand

Penguin Books Ltd, Registered Offices: Harmondsworth, Middlesex, England

First published by Dutton, an imprint of New American Library,
a division of Penguin Books USA Inc.

Distributed in Canada by McClelland & Stewart Inc.

First Printing, April, 1991
10 9 8 7 6 5 4 3 2 1

LIBRARY OF CONGRESS CATALOGING-IN-PUBLICATION DATA
Read, Doris, 1916–
    The Lydia chronicles / Doris Read.
        p.   cm.
    I. Title.
    PS3568.E223L95 1991
    813'.54—dc20   90–46802
                                                        CIP

Printed in the United States of America
Set in Palatino
Designed by Julian Hamer

PUBLISHER'S NOTE
This is a work of fiction. Names, characters, places, and incidents either are the
product of the author's imagination or are used fictitiously, and any resemblance
to actual persons, living or dead, events, or locales is entirely coincidental.

For Steve, John, and Tom
with love

ACKNOWLEDGMENTS

I wish to thank the Santa Barbara City College for their sponsorship of a Writers' Workshop, led by the late Herbert Dalmas, in their Continuing Education Division. This is where *The Lydia Chronicles* first made its appearance. Mr. Dalmas's encouragement and advice were extremely helpful. A few of the chapters were previously published in *Seniority* magazine.

Contents

1

Living Like Movie Stars

One day I said, "Lydia, if you had the sense you were born with you would say good-bye to Illinois and to Miss Swanson, and set out in search of a new life, or at least some high jinks."

I was talking to myself again, as widows sometimes do, and, as usual, what I said seemed remarkably perceptive. Who else, after all, could know that under my drab exterior, longing to get out, was a blonde in jeans and a turtleneck shirt, driving a sports car into the sunset?

I pushed the button that, with wonderful magic, caused the garage door to fly up and hide under the roof. Inside, Miss Swanson, a hefty Buick, crouched sullenly. She was dark green, as ponderous and forbidding as my high school Latin teacher, for whom she was named.

"Miss Swanson," I said, "you have worn out your welcome. You will have to go."

She glared.

"It's a question of survival," I said. "I must be ruthless."

In dignity and silence we proceeded downtown to an auto dealer. I left Miss Swanson in his care.

"Be kind to her," I said, patting her hood. "She has served me well."

Sometimes I wish that I did not develop such intense relationships with my cars. It makes the inevitable parting so painful. I turned away quickly, beat off feelings of guilt, and went home in a new yellow two-seater.

My friend Georgene at La Beau Salonne (I never had the heart to correct Georgene's French, because of the expense of altering the sign) expressed approval of my decision and vanished into the rear of her establishment, where she stirred up some chemicals that made blonde happen. But, as she put it, une blonde discreet.

At a shop called Kool Pants, which I entered through the back door from the parking lot, hoping no one I knew would notice, I acquired suitable garments. I informed Julie, my daughter in Ohio, of my plans, silenced her disapproving squawks by saying "Good-bye, darling. I'll send my address when I get one," and hung up. Then I turned my house over to tenants and drove west into the sunset.

Even with dark glasses, all those sunsets were giving me a permanent squint, so that by the time I arrived in Los Barcos I decided to stop driving and stay a while. I rented an apartment that afforded a glimpse of the ocean if I stood on a chair and twisted my head sideways.

Then I set out to explore the community and discovered several interesting facts. One, that when the pittosporum trees were in bloom, the city smelled as though Chanel Number Five had rained on it. Two, that the streets were full of citizens of venerable age, many in picturesque costumes, revealing their zest for life, California style. Three, that I was lonely, which was not surprising, considering that I didn't know anyone in Los Barcos, but had happened on it purely by chance.

It was Saturday night. I decided to enlarge my experience by going to a singles bar, where I might meet kindred souls. There were, however, a few problems. To begin with, how to distinguish a singles bar from any other kind. What to wear. And would they let me in? I knew that no one under eighteen would be admitted, but how about older girls like me? Would I be turned away at the entrance, like Granny seeking to swim in the kiddy pool? The more I

examined the prospect, the less attractive it became. I changed my mind and planned instead
to participate in a bird-walk early Sunday morning. The paper said Public Invited, and gave the
name of the park.

Some people had already gathered when I
arrived at seven the next morning. A chattering
group of buxom ladies, slung about with binoculars and satchels, stood at the side of the road.
A white-haired man waited in his car, which
bore an uncanny resemblance to Miss Swanson.
I scooted into a parking place beside him.

He climbed down, displaying Animal World
sneakers, came over, and said his name was
John Herman but his friends called him Herm,
and was I there for the bird-walk. I said I was.
He said perhaps I would like to look through his
binoculars if we saw some interesting birds and
I said that was very kind of him. Later I learned
that the sneakers had been purchased for one
dollar, at a Giant Markdown Sale, by Herm's
son Mike, whose wife wouldn't let him wear
them.

Take it from me, when it comes to engaging a
girl's interest, a pair of binoculars in the woods
has it all over an apartment full of etchings.
Before the bird-walk was over, we had a date
for that evening.

Three months later we were sitting in a water-front restaurant.

I said, "Oh Herm, you're so sweet," and reached across the white tablecloth to take his hand. "But I can't marry you."

Herm's long, thin face got longer and thinner. "Why not?" he said. "I think we get along very well."

"Oh yes, that's true," I said.

"And we're both lonely."

"Lonely doesn't begin to describe it," I said.

"I'd try to make you happy, Lydia."

Outside the restaurant window lay never-never-land, with a row of palm trees defining the curve of the shore road. Herm was teaching me the names of the local trees.

"*Washingtonia filifera*," I said, stalling for time.

"Does that mean yes?"

I tilted my head back and half-closed my eyes, in an effort to look like a glamor queen and give Herm the benefit of the frosted eye shadow I had bought that morning. He chose to ignore it. I came back to earth.

"If I remarry," I said, "I'll lose my little tiny pension."

"What shall we do?" he said.

Herm can look gloomier than anybody I have ever known. It is something about the way his features are put together.

I gestured to the scene outside the window.

"Well," I said, "here we are in movie country. Why don't we just live like movie stars? We could have an LTA."

"I don't know what that is," Herm said, "and knowing you, I'm almost afraid to ask."

"It means Living Together Arrangement, Herm. Lots of retired people do it, not only movie stars. Except for the ones who pretend to be brother and sister. The retirement communities are full of them."

"I never heard of such a thing!"

"That's because you always have your head in the trees looking for birds. Did you really believe that Carol Riggin is Art Newcomb's sister?"

"Of course. Otherwise she would call herself Mrs. Newcomb."

"No. This way she can keep her own name. Much simpler all round."

"But everyone knows you're not my sister."

"Oh yes. We can't do *that*. But we *could* have an LTA."

Herm already looked less gloomy but not entirely convinced.

"What would our friends think?" he said. "It's one thing to talk about movie stars, but you know that people here are very conventional."

"Only your fuddy-duddy friends at the Lunch

Club. *My* friends are all back East and they'd think it was great."

I kept my fingers crossed as I said that, just in case.

"Anyway," I said, "we don't have to tell them, do we?"

"Living alone is hell," Herm said.

"Some people like it. Even prefer it," I said. "More freedom."

"That kind of freedom's not so wonderful."

"It has advantages," I said. "But I've been a failure as a widow. No talent for it."

Herm actually smiled.

"There's a bird-walk scheduled for tomorrow," he said, "but we'd better go and look at houses instead."

The house we found was minuscule, but it had a balcony, a view from every room, and an undeveloped garden large enough to keep Herm occupied for years. Herm's idea of heaven is a lot of trees full of unusual birds, right next to an expanse of rich soil where he can crawl around and plant things. The address was propitious—10 Plaza de los Rosales, which nobody can pronounce, so it is commonly known as Rosebush Plaza. Actually, it is not a plaza at all, only a tiny dead-end street, and there were no rosebushes until Herm planted half a dozen, letting me choose the variety. I chose Peace because it is magnificent and the name augured well for a harmonious future.

We arranged to move in on July 1.

"Now," I said, one evening in June, "we must send out cunningly worded announcements."

We made them ourselves, printing At Home across the top, and then stating only our names, our new address, and the date, July 4, which we chose because it would be easy to remember. Interpretation would be up to the recipient.

An assortment of casseroles, place mats, and congratulatory notes arrived, followed by seven people who turned up on the evening of the fourth, under the impression that they had been invited to view the fireworks from our balcony.

Fortunately we had crackers and cheese on hand, but the drinks cupboard was not yet properly stocked. I combined canned beer with ginger ale, in a rough approximation of shandy, a British concoction of dubious merit.

"How clever of you, Lydia," one of our guests said, after tasting it, "to remind us, in this way, of how essential it was that we declare our independence from Britain."

"Herm and I are nothing if not patriotic," I said, smugly.

That was the beginning of our life together. Eminently satisfactory so far, although just the other night, when I served a new, only slightly exotic dish for dinner, Herm put on his most gloomy expression.

"I was warned," he said. "After you mixed up that shandy, I should have known that living with you would be dangerous for my stomach."

But a few minutes later he held out his plate and said, "Is there any more of this whatever you call it, Sugar?"

This morning I bought some gold eyeshadow. Herm bought a new weed puller. Living like movie stars is terrific.

2

The Rock Garden

The McVittys next door on the east, an elfin couple in their seventies, decided to redecorate their kitchen. They bought some wallpaper and came round to ask if they could borrow Herm's tall ladder.

Herm spends a lot of time pretending to be an old man, but he feels young compared with Mr. McVitty, so of course he offered to help them do the high parts. And then, of course, he fell off the ladder and broke his leg in two places. The McVittys found someone down the street whose gardener's nephew wanted a temporary job, and proceeded with their project. Herm and his cast were installed on our sofa and I, Lydia, was forced to take over the gardening so that Herm's precious roses would at least survive, if not flourish.

I know a lot about gardening. I know it ruins

your hands and breaks your back. The hot sun gives you a complexion like Pruneface and dries your hair to straw. Worst of all, there is no permanence about it. The minute you plant something, it either starts to grow or starts to die, usually the latter in my case, but in any event it requires continual attention. It is like dusting the furniture. The specks start falling on it again the instant you walk away. I much prefer painting, which allows you a moment of triumph each time you create something and can look at it with pride and say, "It's finished." Gardening is never finished.

I puttered around for a while, under Herm's direction, and tried to keep things tidy. Then one day I discovered that we had been invaded by a creeping evil called Bermuda grass. It was coming in, maliciously, most likely, from our neighbors on the west, two couples who share a house and a machine that causes our walls to vibrate as, for hours at a time, it pounds and howls with an insistent percussive beat. We tried to ignore it and shut it out by closing our windows. Herm has suggested that these people belong to one of those exotic cults described in the news magazines, especially when we observed that the din was often accompanied by black smoke and the stench of burning grease, as they engaged in a curious ritual of consecrating red meat over fire and then forcing themselves to eat the charred remains. There is a hole in the hedge, made by their dog, and I must confess we have peeked through. We have not complained of either the noise or the smell because such people move frequently and we don't expect to have them for long as neighbors.

However, with Herm confined to the house, unable to escape either the smell of the burnt offerings or the accompanying sound effects from the machine, the situation became critical. A weekend of nonstop devotions next door was the last straw. Herm exploded on Sunday afternoon.

"I can't stand it any more," he said. "You phone them right now, Lydia, and tell them your husband is in great pain, suffering, whatever you can think of, and must have peace and quiet."

I was less than eager to do this.

"You're not in great pain, Herm."

He groaned dramatically.

"*Please*, Lydia."

"It's getting late," I said. "I'm sure they'll stop soon."

"But they'll start again in the morning," Herm said.

"No they won't. Tomorrow's Monday and they all go to work."

Herm groaned again. As though in response, the racket from next door grew louder. The rites were evidently approaching a climax, and new clouds of smoke drifted through our windows. I consulted the telephone directory but although the name on their mailbox was Bewley, the only Bewley listed lived on the other side of town.

"Well then, go over and ring their bell and tell them," Herm said.

He sounded so desperate that I capitulated.

"If I'm not back in ten minutes, you'll know I've been offered up," I said.

As I approached the Bewleys' front door the noise was mind-blowing but I found the doorbell and rang. Nothing happened. I tried again, leaning on the button. Still nothing. It occurred to me that they might not be able to hear the bell and the only way to get their attention would be to go around to the back of the house where the ceremonies were taking place. No, I could not do it.

I went home and explained this to Herm, adding that I was ashamed of my cowardice but there it was.

At nine-thirty in the evening the worshippers decided that their gods were propitiated for the time being. The machine was switched off and the fire extinguished. Herm and I looked at each other and recited in unison: Silence, like a poultice, comes to heal the wounds of sound.

"I'll write a note," Herm said, "and you can leave it in their mailbox tomorrow."

In the morning I prepared to deal with the Bermuda grass. You can't poison it without killing everything else in the area. All you can do is dig it up, bit by bit, day after day, pulling at the horrible writhing roots that will start to grow again the minute you straighten up. I decided to attack it with a hoe.

"Take that, and *that*, and THAT!" I shouted as I whacked the filthy stuff. "Take *that*, you obscene obscenity!"

Now I want to make it clear that I am, most of the time, a well-behaved person, never completely recovered from the years when, before I left the house, some adult would check to make sure I was wearing gloves and carrying a clean handkerchief. Uninhibited profanity was not my style. But I seemed to have a talent for it. If I couldn't think of any good bad words, I made them up.

"A thousand curses on you and all your blank blank blankety relations!" I was screaming, brandishing a choice root two feet long and richly branched, when I became aware that I was not alone. I tried to straighten up by leaning heavily on the hoe, and, upright at last, confronted the horrified faces of two female missionaries in the driveway. One of them managed a smile and held out a pamphlet.

"Perhaps this would help you," she said, "in your search for God. We can all be saved."

I would have taken the pamphlet, just to be polite, but had no free hand.

"It's too late for me," I said. "But thank you just the same."

They left reluctantly. I must confess I was shaken. I had never thought about being overheard. I put away the hoe and staggered back to the house. Herm's note was still in my pocket because a car in the Bewleys' driveway indicated that they had not all left the house and I preferred to wait until they had done so before approaching.

Herm, lolling like a sultan on the sofa, was reading a detective story and polishing off a plate of chocolate cookies brought by Mrs. McVitty. She feels somehow responsible for his accident and brings him goodies almost every day. He is getting fat.

"What's for lunch?" he inquired. Poor lamb, he is so bored.

I fetched the sherry and a couple of glasses.

"The swearing will have to stop," I told him.

"I'm glad to hear it," he said. "You're really not the type."

Later in the afternoon, when I had regained my strength, I went out again to the battlefield. At almost the same moment, the owners of the machine turned it on at high volume. Out of the windows poured the sound. BOOM wah wah wah BOOM wah wah wah. The rhythm was perfect. I banged down the hoe on each BOOM and straightened up on the wah wah wahs. Fury gave me the necessary energy. This was better than swearing.

I was well into this when Herm's granddaughter Sandra came along. Since the accident, she sometimes comes by after school to cheer him up. She stopped in the driveway to greet me and we stood silent in the flood of BOOM wah from next door.

"Hey Lydia, you've got it made," she shouted. "Doing the gardening and listening to Jimi Hendrix at the same time."

"You mean that noise is something admirable?"

"Oh man!" She rolled her eyes for emphasis.

I paused to consider this. Mozart, of course, is my idol, as he is of every civilized person, but let's face it, Mozart was not helping me with the Bermuda grass. Besides, once you stop having an open mind, you might as well buy a Whistler's Mother chair and spend the rest of your life in it. Knitting booties.

"What name did you say?"

"Jimi Hendrix. One of the greatest in hard rock," she said, and continued up to the house.

I thought about this as I put in a last few whacks with the hoe and decided that I could admit Jimi Hendrix into my life, at least on a limited basis. Before entering the house, I stopped by the trash can and dropped in Herm's note. If any notes are written and delivered, I decided, they would be thank-you notes. And that is how Herm's rose bed, free now of Bermuda grass, became known as the rock garden.

3

The Cow

Certainly the affair of the cow was not at all the sort of fracas that Herm and I would normally become involved in. One day, however, a heavy hand on the doorbell disrupted the tranquility of our cocktail hour, which is devoted to the reading of the newspaper while sipping a modest potation.

The bell rang twice before I could get to it, although I move pretty fast. Mr. Gudge, our neighbor, whose back garden faces us directly across the street, stood there flourishing a petition.

The petition was addressed to the Mayor, Members of the City Council, and the Architectural Board of Review. It requested the removal of the cow on top of the Dimple Dairy building, at the intersection of Via La Loma, which winds down our hill, with Ribera Street, the somewhat

seedy main thoroughfare at the bottom, on the grounds that it was unesthetic, dangerous, irrelevant, and constituted an attractive nuisance.

Its esthetic value was a matter of personal taste, but it could be argued that it was dangerous because it might fall over into the street during an earthquake; irrelevant because the Dimple Dairy had long been defunct and the building now housed several small businesses, including a hot dog emporium called Dimple Dogs, to accord with the words "Dimple Building" cut into the facade over the main entrance; and an attractive nuisance because the high school students who patronized Dimple Dogs and the other nearby fast-food establishments were in the habit of climbing up onto the flat roof of the building (it was only one story high) and painting the cow in different colors and designs every few days. During the football season, exhortations to the team would be printed on the boxlike structure supporting the cow, and she herself might wear a football helmet on her patient head; sometimes she was painted in stripes like a zebra; sometimes in assorted colors—red legs, green body, blue udder, white head; sometimes all one color but spotted as though she had a case of giant measles. The painting was done secretly, at night. The proprietor of Dimple Dogs, delighted by the free publicity and increased business as a result of the cow on his roof, even provided a ladder.

Herm and I always enjoyed stopping at the traffic light there, on our way downtown, to see the latest product of the kids' imagination. We felt that the cow was surely a source of innocent merriment and could not understand why anyone would object to it. In our opinion, it was one of the few bright spots on Ribera Street.

I invited Mr. Gudge in, offered him a drink, which he first refused, then accepted, and we all sat down around the coffee table to discuss the matter of the cow.

We have several neighbors who test severely our love for our fellow man. The blaring hi-fi and barbecue people next door, for example, and Mr. Gudge, who buys broken-down trucks and cars, parks them in the street behind his house, which unfortunately is directly in front of *our* house, and works on them for weeks, so that the street is littered with odd bits of automotive hardware, and banging and revving up of engines can be heard at all hours. Then, presumably, he sells the reconditioned vehicle and we have a few weeks' respite until he gets another one. He has a wife, who can sometimes be seen walking around in the garden, but I have never spoken with her.

After some discussion, it came to light that

Mrs. Gudge had rented a small shop, where she proposed to set up an interior decorating business, on Ribera Street across from the Dimple Building. Judging by what I could see of the Gudge interior when driving by at night, Mrs. Gudge was not really fitted for this line of work, but *de gustibus non disputandum*. She was convinced that the presence of the cow on the roof would detract from the dignity and elegance of her establishment, and in fact, that it lowered the tone of the whole area. She had drawn up the petition and persuaded her husband to circulate it.

He had started only that afternoon, but already had about a dozen signatures. I looked them over. One was that of a bad-tempered woman at the end of the block. I was at the mailbox when she stopped her car one day and complained that ours was an ugly house, in her opinion. One signature was that of a foreign-born woman whose husband taught at the college but who, herself, had only a limited grasp of English and could not possibly have understood what Mr. Gudge was talking about. Several signatures were those of the Gudges' friends and relations who lived in the vicinity, and one, I was not surprised to see, was that of a Hollywoodish couple in dark glasses who roared in and out of our little street in their Porsche, and kept a vicious dog, which was allowed to roam at large and terrorize people. It was because of this animal that I refused to go around collecting for diseases. I think they kept calling me because nobody else would do it either, for the same reason. There was no use calling the dogcatcher. He said he would come only if we caught the dog and held him in custody.

"I'm sorry, Mr. Gudge," I said, handing back the petition, "but I can't possibly sign this."

"Why don't you circulate a petition asking the city to provide a street light on this block?" Herm said. "*That* would make some sense."

"Some kid might fall off that roof and get killed," Gudge argued, but we were unmoved. Compared with drug taking, reckless driving, and hang gliding, painting the cow seemed a harmless amusement.

The local newspaper sent a reporter to interview the Gudges, and then ran the piece under a headline "Threat To Children's Safety." Letters to the Editor, pro and con, appeared. The local authorities, however, were up to their necks in hearings concerning the renovation of the town center, which would involve razing most of the old buildings and replacing them with new ones designed to look like coffee cans, the circular motif being now fashionable. The Gudges began to see the affair as their personal crusade, protecting the children against public apathy.

Mrs. Gudge was busy getting her shop organized. She hoped to open for business before Christmas, in case someone wanted to get spruced up for the holidays. She had gold lettering painted on the shop window: Gloria's Grotto for Gracious Interiors. Occasionally she would appear in the doorway and glare at the cow and at the lunchtime groups of teenagers milling around beneath it while eating Dimple Dogs.

Herm's granddaughter Sandra stopped by one day after school.

"Can't you do something, Grampa? Lydia?" she asked. "Talk to Mrs. Gudge or something?"

I pointed out that we had never had what might be called cordial relations with the Gudges, and now that we had refused to sign the petition, Mr. Gudge would no longer even say good morning when we went in and out of our driveway, but retreated under the hood of the car he was working on and pretended not to see us. We promised to think about it.

The football season drew to a close. The city authorities festooned the downtown lampposts with artificial holly wreaths and limp red plastic bows, and the merchants arranged for seasonal music to pour forth into the streets. It was a clever ploy. Driven off the streets by the din, citizens fled into the shops and bought things they might not otherwise have known they wanted, lingering inside as long as possible to avoid the attack on their ears.

I had an idea, which I communicated to Sandra. She conferred with her fellows at the high school, and reported enthusiastic approval.

So it was that, two weeks before Christmas, Herm and I drove down the hill, stopped at the traffic light, and looked across the street at the cow. Gone was the football regalia. She was now red all over, with golden horns. A huge wreath of pine branches, cones, and scarlet berries hung around her neck. On the white box beneath her were the words, in red, "Merry Christmas to Ribera St. and esp. Welcome greetings to Gloria's Grotto." Because of the length of the message, it went around three sides of the box, but the printing was large and clear; and the words "Gloria's Grotto" had been done in green to make them stand out.

Mrs. Gudge accepted defeat. She wrote a Letter to the Editor publicly thanking the high school students for their friendly gesture. The petition was withdrawn.

Yesterday, when we drove down the hill, we noticed that the cow had been painted white, with a big red heart on either flank. Valentine's Day is approaching.

4

The Hawks

After less than a year, Herm and I were quarreling. We sat at the breakfast table and snarled at each other, until Herm jumped up and marched away. I sat there eating kippers, a delicacy that Herm has not yet learned to appreciate.

After breakfast, I found him in the patio, where he was pouring too much water on some sickly plants. This proved he was upset, because Herm is a good gardener. He scowled at me.

"Those pants are too tight. I wish you'd stop wearing them," he said.

But I had rehearsed my speech and was determined not to be sidetracked.

"It is unseemly and ridiculous," I said, "at our age, not to be able to get along peacefully."

"It's not ridiculous," said Herm, drowning a

potted azalea. "I thought we were both looking for companionship."

"Of course," I agreed.

"I was very lonely after Alice died."

"Yes. I know how it is."

"I was in a deep depression."

"I know."

"I thought we could help each other. I thought you would want to share my life."

"I do, Herm. Of course I do. But not twenty-four hours a day every day. There are other things I have to do."

"You don't *have* to. You *want* to. Don't you realize we are retired now?"

"I haven't retired from life," I said.

I watched his face droop into pitiful folds. He fished around in his private pool of misery, and, having hooked something, he dredged it up and presented it dripping wet.

"I can't understand it," he said. "Alice and I never quarreled. In thirty years we never had words." He was silent for a moment. "I guess she was an angel."

"Must have been," I said, and went inside, slamming the kitchen door.

For the rest of the day a grim silence prevailed at 10 Rosebush Plaza. Herm set out for his daily walk without me, wearing the expression of a convicted criminal starting on the last mile. I holed up in my studio, sitting in front of my canvas pretending to paint, and carrying on imaginary arguments with Herm.

"How could you possibly expect me to be like Alice?" I said. "I am Lydia. I couldn't be like Alice even if I wanted to, which I don't."

I snatched up my drawing pad and drew a stick figure with enormous wings and a sausage-curled head tapering to a receding chin. It needed something more, so I added prissy pink lips. I labeled it Alice the Angel. When I looked at it I became angry again, this time angry with myself for doing such a hateful thing. I tore the paper into tiny bits.

At lunch time Herm made a peanut butter sandwich and took it to the far corner of the garden. When I went to the kitchen I discovered that he had used some stale bread that I was saving for casserole crumbs. I made another sandwich for him and took it out with a glass of milk on a tray.

Herm was sitting morosely under the pepper tree, holding his stale sandwich and looking at it as though it contained worms. I took it from his hand, set down the tray, and returned to the house. Neither of us said a word.

By cocktail time we were both exhausted.

"I think we should consult someone," I suggested.

"Either that, or break it off," Herm said. "I was planning to leave in the morning."

"Where would you go?" I asked him, genuinely curious.

"I'd find a place," Herm said. "And then I'd come back for my clothes and you wouldn't have to bother about me any more."

He really meant it!

"The Ottersons went to a Dr. Bell. I'll call him in the morning," I said.

Dr. Bell, smooth and rotund, sat in a swivel chair facing us. The sun poured in on his bald head, making him look like a Buddha.

"What it boils down to," I said, "is that Herm wishes to become an Old Man. Professionally. With me as full-time attendant. And I won't have it. It's not as though he were sick or something."

"Oh?" said Dr. Bell, expertly laconic.

I plunged ahead. It was now or never.

"He resents any interest of mine that doesn't coincide with his own. I mean, I enjoy going on bird-walks with him, but I need to do other things too. I'm studying painting at the Institute and that's very important to me. Herm is jealous."

Dr. Bell swiveled toward Herm and raised his eyebrows.

"That's an exaggeration," Herm said. "We really get along very well most of the time. We are very fond of each other."

Dr. Bell said nothing. There was a long pause.

"I guess I thought Lydia would want to be with me instead of spending so much time at that art school. It's not as though she—"

He trailed off, on the verge of saying something unforgivable.

I glared at him.

"My talent, or lack of it, is beside the point," I said. "I am being smothered by too much togetherness."

Dr. Bell looked right straight at me and smiled.

"Give me room?" he suggested.

Oh, what a lovely man! He understood exactly. I felt a thousand times better.

"Yes. Quite," I said.

"Come back in a couple of weeks," Dr. Bell said.

We climbed into my car and started home. It was a beautiful day. I felt conciliatory.

"You know," I said to Herm, "it's always difficult for a woman to get used to having a retired man around all day. Even when it's the man she's spent most of her life with. Which is not our case."

Herm said nothing.

"Of course," I went on, "as Ann Landers says, there are plenty of women who would be glad to have such a problem. Don't think I'm not aware of that."

Someone started to back out of a driveway in front of us.

"Watch out!" Herm yelled.

I had already braked. I am training myself to ignore Herm's backseat driving. What can't be cured must be endured, my grandmother used to say.

"Herm, let's take a sandwich up to the mountains. It's really a good day."

He brightened at that. Herm adores picnics. Sometimes, when he isn't working at being an old man, he is very like a small boy.

"What about your art class?"

This was to show me that the truce was still uncertain.

"I don't have one on Wednesdays."

We took a road that leads out of town into the hills and through a pass to the valley beyond. Herm was driving his old car. He never talks much when he drives. I examined the scenery and thought about how nice it would be up here if only we weren't mad at each other. I pointed to the ubiquitous chaparral and attempted a small bon mot.

"Could be called 'Infinite Variations on Green.' "

Herm grunted.

We drove along the crest until he spotted a

clearing with scattered oaks. We sat on rocks eating our sandwiches and watching the horses and cows in the valley below. Afterward, we slung on our binoculars and started to walk down the side of the road.

"Wrong time of day for birds," Herm grumbled, peering into the trees along the road.

We saw only a flock of bushtits working over a large manzanita and a jay squawking from the top of an oak.

Herm came to such a sudden stop that I bumped into him. He trained his binoculars on the sky, where a tiny spot appeared to be coming closer.

"It's a hawk!"

"What kind, Herm?"

"Not sure yet."

It is exciting to see hawks. They appeal to an atavistic side of our natures, a fearful secret admiration for the raptor. My arms began to ache from the strain of holding up the binoculars.

The hawk came closer.

"Herm, look! There are two of them!"

"A pair of redtails," Herm said. "Sometimes you see them together. Not often."

The hawks flew side by side for a moment. Then they separated and began to describe large figure-eights in the sky, flying away from each other, then curving back to close the circle, cross over, and circle again in the opposite direction. They rose higher, their fanned-out tails as red as copper with the sun shining through. Then they vanished.

We lowered our binoculars and walked on. I thought about the hawks.

"Herm," I said, "did you notice the pattern the hawks made? He went in one direction and she in another, and then they came back together again, and then apart, and then together. That's the way it should be for us, Herm."

"Yuh," Herm said, and kept walking.

In my mind, I could still see the hawks.

"They are really with each other all the time, in spirit, I mean," I said.

Herm did not respond. I wondered if my words had blown past him unheard, but then he turned and held out his hand. I grasped it and together we walked back to the car.

5

A Two-Way Street

Herm is not only an excellent gardener, but also a man of strong character. No nonsense about saving little bits and pieces of anything. What is pruned off or chopped down goes immediately into the compost heap or a trash bag. He is always delighted to give anyone who asks cuttings from a plant, but he will not go around offering them gratuitously. I admire him for this and wish I could do likewise.

While the garden is solely Herm's responsibility, the houseplants and the pots on the little balcony are mine. Like every householder who gives shelter to a potted plant, I often find myself in the same position as the owner of an unspayed female cat, begging friends to take some of the abundant progeny.

That was how the trouble started.

It began with the jade plants, *Crassula argentea*.

They are thick-leaved succulents that thrive any-where and have the capacity for surviving even the most callous neglect. If happy, they will put forth flowers. After a while, they become un-gainly and top-heavy. They threaten to split the pots that once seemed so spacious but now look like thimbles under the mass of foliage. I pray for strength of mind and fetch the pruning shears. It is always a time of sorrow.

A few months ago I had to endure one of these traumatic experiences and ended up, as usual, with a basket full of lively jade-plant cut-tings. Herm came out on the balcony and said, "Shall I dump these in the trash can for you?"

I should have let him do it. Instead, I stood protectively in front of the basket and assured Herm that I knew lots of people who would be glad to have the cuttings. When he had gone, I sat down and tried to think of who they might be.

My friend Poppy was out of the running, as she had been the recipient of the preceding batch; she was now herself playing the role of Lady Bountiful. Sue Jenkins specialized in fancy gera-niums for the sunny places and fancy begonias for the shade; she would not accept a jade plant. Mr. McVitty next door had been working on his garden for so many years that every inch of it was allocated to something he treasured and there was no room for anything else. Shirley had just moved to an apartment and, weeping, had to dispose of most of her plants. Our rock music neighbors were not interested in gardening, and anyway, I would rather kill the plants myself, giving them a quick and merciful death, than turn them over to suffer in that noisy smoke-filled backyard. While I was brooding over this, the phone rang.

"It's for you, Lydia," Herm called, and I went inside.

The caller was Mrs. Honeycott, the awe-inspiring barrel-shaped founder and director of our local choral society. Although I am not a member of the group, Mrs. Honeycott sometimes bullies me into playing accompaniments for them.

"It would be only two rehearsals, Lydia," she wheedled. "Surely you could fit that in. I would appreciate it so much."

She did not, of course, take into account the time I would have to spend learning the accompaniment, which would probably be dull and difficult. I was hemming and hawing when the light bulb flashed in my head.

"Well, all right, if it's only two rehearsals," I said. "By the way, would you like some cuttings from my jade plants? I've just pruned them."

"How nice, dear. I'll send Fernando (her gardener) over with the music and he can pick them up."

I felt that I was paying a high price to get a home for the jade plants, but it was worth it. I wrapped the best cuttings in wet newspaper, put the whole thing into a plastic bag to await the coming of Fernando, and delivered the rest to Herm.

"Please dispose of them, darling, but don't tell me about it," I said.

Fernando came. I practiced the accompaniments to some thoroughly dreary songs, which meant I had no time for the Mozart sonata I was trying to learn, but it was all in a good cause.

Two days after the performance, Fernando appeared at our door with a plastic bag twice the size of the one I had given him.

"Mrs. Honeycott she say to give you these," he announced, handed me the bag, and ran back to his truck as though pursued.

The bag contained a dozen baby spider plants that Fernando had lovingly planted in tiny plastic pots of various colors. I lined them up on the balcony floor where we kept tripping over them. It was the beginning of a nightmare.

Two weeks later Fernando returned with a sack of geranium cuttings. I was ready for him with two chunks hacked off an overgrown rubber plant, and a divided asparagus fern.

"Things are getting a little crowded around here," I told Fernando, when he appeared again two weeks later with an assortment of lavender chrysanthemums which I knew Herm would refuse to plant in the garden because of their depressing color.

"I know," Fernando said. "But Mrs. Honeycott, she say you must take."

I gave him a bag of philodendron pieces and he left.

As soon as he was out of sight, not giving myself time to think of how wickedly destructive I was being, I carried the chrysanthemums to the trash can and dropped them in.

This simple act produced a spasm of intense euphoria. I considered it for all of two minutes and remembered my grandmother, who was given to homely proverbs, saying "Strike while the iron is hot."

I found a large grocery sack and went out to the balcony. In went all the spider plants, one after the other. I didn't even try to save the little plastic pots, knowing that during the time required to remove the plants, my resolve might weaken. The geraniums, still sitting in a pail of water, went in next. The pail could then be put away. Suddenly the balcony looked wide and serene.

"Eureka!" I shouted.

Herm, out in the garden fussing with his roses, looked up, startled, but was too busy to comment.

Of course it had to happen that Mrs. Honeycott herself would eventually turn up at our house. She came one day with some music that she asked me to deliver to Poppy, who sings in the chorus.

"I know you see her frequently," Mrs. Honeycott said, "and you know I live clear across town and Poppy wasn't home just now and I do want her to have it."

I agreed to deliver the music.

"You must have a splendid view from your balcony," Mrs. Honeycott said, sneakily.

What could I do?

"Do please come in and look," I said.

We went through the house and out to the balcony. Mrs. Honeycott admired the view, which is quite good, and then she looked around at my potted plants.

"I thought perhaps you would have the spider plants out here," she said. "They are so good on a balcony. And where did you put the geraniums?"

"I know it's hard to believe," I said, "but they all died. I planted them so carefully but I think it's too hot or too cold or too windy or something, out here."

Mrs. Honeycott looked as though she didn't believe a word of it.

"And besides," I added, "I don't like to tell people, but the fact is, I have a black thumb. When I touch a plant, it's the kiss of death."

I tried to look mournful as I told this whopper.

Mrs. Honeycott, to my amazement, gave me a warm smile.

"Don't worry about it, Lydia my dear," she said. "I'm sure it's not as bad as you think. I'll send Fernando over with some more cuttings and you can try again."

"How kind of you!" I said. "And maybe in exchange you could use some of this sansevieria which has to be divided."

We beamed at each other with complete understanding, and she left.

Our arrangement has been fantastically successful. Every few weeks Fernando appears with a sack of cuttings, and I hand him one of mine, and then I telephone Mrs. Honeycott and we thank each other. It says in the Bible that it is more blessed to give than to receive, but Mrs. Honeycott and I know better. Giving and receiving —it's a two-way street.

6

Doing the Thing

Herm and I were enjoying our predinner drink and reading the evening paper when my eye was caught by a department store ad. Perhaps it was the effect of the cocktail, but without consciously planning to do so, I found myself saying, "Herm, I have just made an irreversible decision."

Herm hates to be interrupted when he is reading the paper, but he looked up politely and said, "You have?"

"Yes. Hamilton's is having a special on Friday afternoon. They pierce your ears and give you a pair of earrings, all for a modest sum."

"Are you sure you want to do this?"

"I've been thinking about it a long time."

"But you've always said—"

"I've changed my mind. Poppy and I are the only women in town with old-fashioned ears."

"My grandmother had pierced ears," Herm said. "She was not exactly an up-to-date person."

I waved it away.

"Oh your grandmother, my grandmother, everybody's grandmother. That has nothing to do with it."

Herm can recognize good solid logic when he encounters it. He changed direction.

"Who does the piercing?"

He is always suspicious of anything that might constitute illegal or dangerous medical practice.

"A registered nurse, it says here."

"Well, I'll go with you if you like."

Herm is really a sweetie. I was sure he would ask to see the nurse's credentials.

"That would be lovely," I told him. "Only thing is, I want to go and poke around in that fabric shop for an hour or so afterward, so I thought I'd ask Poppy to go with me. She might want to have her ears done too."

The prospect of an hour in the fabric shop was an effective deterrent. Herm conceded to Poppy the position of escort.

To be precise about all this, it was not the decision, but the act, that would be irreversible. Once done, it could not be undone. My problem is that, like Kipling's Elephant's Child, I suffer from insatiable curiosity. I don't want to miss out on anything that is widely hailed as interesting, entertaining, or inspiring. Some experiences, like modern dance, Indian cooking, or group sex, can be tried and, if found wanting, abandoned, with no permanent effects. But if you are persuaded to attempt, for example, mother-hood, because it is something a woman should not miss, you end up, after a good deal of trouble, with a baby. Now there you are with this baby, like it or not. You can, of course, give it away, as some people in desperate circumstances do, but even so drastic an act would not change the fact that you are a mother. It is the same with jumping off a bridge. If you try it and don't like it, it's too late to turn back.

I don't mean to imply that having one's ears pierced is comparable in importance to producing a baby or jumping off a bridge, but it is just as irreversible. You will have holes in your ears, or at least, marks where the holes were, for the rest of your life. But I had dreamed for years of wearing gold gypsy hoops, and the great dramatist Sophocles himself said, "One must learn by doing the thing: . . . you have no certainty, until you try."

Herm says it will take more than gold hoops to make me look like a gypsy, but he simply refuses to see the real me.

I called Poppy after dinner. She readily agreed to go with me, offered to hold my hand and any parcels I might have, but would not, herself, participate.

On the appointed day I dressed soberly, as though going to a funeral or a job interview. A dark suit and careful makeup are a woman's first lines of defense against the unknown. Poppy, being uninvolved, wore a pink pantsuit and a blue headscarf with dog pictures on it.

On the way to Hamilton's it struck me, not for the first time, how much more relaxed I felt driving with Poppy instead of Herm in the passenger seat. Herm is an inveterate backseat driver and I have learned that there is no use protesting when he starts. The anger flares up and I swallow it, after which it lies in my stomach like a ball of lead. But this is something I must live with. Herm is a stubborn man and unlikely to change his ways.

We were the first to arrive at Hamilton's earring counter. The nurse, in white uniform, was busily arranging her equipment on a card table set up in the aisle, between earrings on the one side and pantyhose on the other. A small chair, for the victim, stood beside the card table.

Poppy gasped.

"You mean, they just do it out here, in public?"

"Oh sure," I said. "What did you expect?"

"Well, a little private room, or cubbyhole, at least. So you could lie down."

"Nonsense," I said.

It is good to have a dithery friend like Poppy. She makes me overcome my own fears in order to still hers.

The nurse turned around and I knew her face

was familiar, but I couldn't place her. She directed me to the counter where the salesgirl was preparing a form for me to sign.

Poppy, having inspected the nurse's table, was more dithery than ever.

"What's that for, Lydia?" she said, peering over my shoulder.

"This absolves them of any responsibility in case my ears fall off," I told her, as I signed my name, attributing the shaky writing to the salesgirl's faulty pen rather than my own nervous condition.

I looked at the nurse again. Where had I seen her before? That frizzy gray hair with the black patch in front, on one side. The tubby shape. The wide smile.

"Have you ever worked at Pacific Hospital?" I asked her.

"Yes! Yes! And you are Mrs. Herman. Mr. Herman had the broken leg. I'll never forget him!"

She rolled her eyes and laughed.

"You're Mrs. Carberry!"

"Yes, yes. And how is your husband?"

"Fine, fine, thank you. You were so good to him in the hospital."

She beamed.

"You're not at the hospital any more?"

"No, I've retired. I just do part-time jobs like this. But I miss the hospital, you know. All those nice people, like Mr. Herman."

A group of piercees was gathering, mostly young and wearing jeans. It was time for action.

I handed Poppy my handbag and sat on the chair, feeling like the central figure at a public execution. The waiting customers and a few passersby gathered around, frankly staring. Mrs. Carberry made a mark on each of my ears, and with a little gun, pop! shot a piercing stud into the left one.

The next in line, a mousy girl, leaned over, breathless.

"Did it hurt?"

I had jumped, I know I had, but perhaps not high enough to notice.

"Oh no," I lied.

A large middle-aged woman stopped in the aisle and did a double take.

"Why Mrs. Herman! My goodness! How do you like your new machine?"

"Mrs. Watkins! The machine is just great."

It was the saleslady who had recently persuaded me to buy a fancier sewing machine than I really needed, but I did not hold it against her. I have a weakness for gadgets and she found me a pushover. She stopped to watch the proceedings.

We now had quite an audience blocking the aisle. Poppy jiggled on the edge of the crowd. She couldn't bear to look, although there was no blood. At least I don't think there was.

Mrs. Carberry popped her gun into the other ear and I stood up.

"Give my regards to your husband," she said to me. "Such a funny man. I'll never forget him!"

She started to laugh again but, realizing that the piercees were waiting, returned to her duties.

Poppy and I went to the fabric shop and finally, home. Herm was reading the paper and waiting for the appearance of the cocktail tray. Relieved to see that I was not noticeably damaged, he resorted to a primitive type of humor he sometimes indulges in.

"You didn't get your money's worth," he said. "Where's the ring in your nose?"

"I go back for that next week," I said. "You'll never guess who the nurse was. Mrs. Carberry!"

Herm looked blank.

"From the hospital. You must have been a real cutup when I wasn't there to see. She told me, twice, that she'll never forget you."

"Is that right?" he said, smirking.

"It was six months ago but she still remembers you."

"Of course."

"What did you do, pinch her?"

"Nothing, I assure you. I think I told her that she was too young and pretty to be waiting on a couple of old fellows like me and that fake cowboy in the other bed. She liked that."

"You old devil," I said.

It always pleases a man to be called an old devil.

I went into the bathroom, looked in the mirror, and returned to Herm.

"You know, I'm not so sure I want to wear earrings all the time, every day and at night, too. Or else the holes close up."

"You should have thought of that before."

"Jean MacGregor told me that, in Scotland, it used to be that earrings were worn only by fallen women."

"That's tough, Sugar."

He rustled the paper and I left him to it.

What's done is done. In six weeks or so I can take out these studs, they tell me, and wear the gold hoops. That is the moment I am waiting for.

Poppy keeps phoning to ask if my ears have fallen off yet.

"Not yet," I tell her. "Besides, as Sophocles says, if you don't live dangerously, you are simply not living at all."

This is, of course, a mad exaggeration of Sophocles' perfectly sensible advice, but with Poppy it is necessary to exaggerate. However, I doubt that she will ever do the thing.

7

Birds of a Feather

Our friend Shirley had been a widow for several years. She is a large woman, tall and cushiony. She colors her hair a rich brown and wears it in a style that was fashionable thirty years ago. Her clothes are expensive and chosen with care, but with her excessive curves she never looks really smart. However, she is a good-natured person with a cheerful attitude toward life, and it was sad to see her floundering in the sea of loneliness into which widows are so heartlessly tossed.

It was all very well, she told me, as though I didn't know it myself, to spend the days in volunteer work at the hospital, club meetings with other women, adult education classes, or just shopping, but the moment would come when she had to go home and open the door to emptiness and solitude. Last year she thought that perhaps there would be less loneliness in a smaller place, so she gave away most of her plants, disposed of some furniture, sold her house, and moved to an apartment. But it made little difference.

We did our best to help her, but the only help she really wanted was to find a new man, and as everyone knows, there are never enough men to go around. Certainly Herm and I didn't know any unattached ones. So we were delighted when we heard that Shirley had acquired a boyfriend, a man she met on a bird-walk.

The fact that she met him on a bird-walk seemed to us a good omen, as that is how Herm and I had met. There is a feeling of intimacy that comes from sharing a pair of binoculars in the woods. It can lead quickly to an even closer relationship. Those who consider bird-watching a yawn-provoking activity, engaged in mainly by elderly eccentrics, are unaware of the titillating possibilities. Furthermore, we were reasonably sure that Shirley had not fallen prey to some scoundrel, because bird-watchers are mostly kind and gentle people. Bird-watching is not a sport that attracts scoundrels because there is no financial or social advantage to be gained.

Alan was a man we could approve of, at least as a companion for Shirley. For one thing, they looked right together. Both were tall, heavy, dignified people. Alan confided to Shirley that he had taken up birding because he thought walking so much outdoors would help him to keep his weight under control. Just plain walking or jogging for exercise was tedious, he said. He liked to have a more entertaining reason for doing it. Shirley agreed. She was charmed by his bushy red moustache, which tickled when he kissed her and more than compensated for the bare space on his head.

After some discussion of whose apartment they should live in, they decided on Alan's because it had a better view. Herm and I gave a small party for them, to launch their new status as a couple. Nothing was said about marriage. Everyone knew perfectly well that among retired people second marriages are frequently LTA's (Living Together Arrangements), because legal marriage would entail financial disaster. It was fun to have a party. I needed an excuse to try making amuse-gueules au Roquefort.

Shirley was the kind of person who preferred to soft-pedal her troubles. She was not a complainer. No doubt that was one thing that attracted Alan in the first place. Sometimes Shirley walked a bit stiffly and I knew her arthritis was bothering her, but I never mentioned it. She would not have liked it. She did exercises every day, she told me once, as the doctor advised, and that, together with some mild medication, enabled her to live normally. As most of the people we know have arthritis, to a lesser or greater degree, it was often a topic of conversation, but not with Shirley.

"So boring, for pity's sake," she would say. "Let's talk about the new exhibition at the Art Center."

And she would shift the focus of attention from illness to art. Herm and I found this admirable, and we wished her much happiness in her new life.

It was a great shock, a few weeks after the party, to meet Shirley for lunch one day and find her wearing dark glasses in an effort to conceal a black eye. I have never understood why this phenomenon is called a "black" eye. It is more likely to be a combination of blue, green, and yellow, accompanied by puffiness. Knowing Shirley's reluctance to admit that anything was wrong with her, I pretended not to notice it, but could hardly wait to get home to tell Herm.

"Poor Shirley!" I said. "She has got herself into the clutches of a brute, a wife-beater. And he seemed such a nice man."

Herm, of course, was appalled by the news.

"I never heard of a bird-watcher who beat up women," he said, "but I guess Alan is the exception that proves the rule."

Word of the black eye got around quickly in our little circle, and, prepared to offer comfort, we all waited for the news that Shirley had left Alan. When we saw him downtown one day, we ostentatiously crossed to the other side of the street.

Two weeks passed. The rainbow around Shirley's right eye gradually faded. She and Alan were seen together at all the usual places. They appeared to be extremely happy. Alan's manner toward Shirley was attentive and affectionate. Perhaps she had just walked into a door.

The next thing that happened was that our friend Poppy had a morning coffee for a visiting cousin, and Shirley turned up with a livid bruise on her right cheekbone. I drew her aside into the hall.

"Shirley," I said, "I know it's none of my business, but your friends are all worried about you and we want you to know that no matter what, we are on your side and furthermore we think you are in danger, living with a man who has fits of violence."

Shirley stared at me and began to laugh.

"You mean this?" she said, pointing to her cheek.

I nodded.

"You think *Alan* did it?"

"And the black eye, too."

She looked both amused and sad.

"I have a real problem, Lydia," she said. "I

guess I'd better tell you. But I don't want Alan to find out. Promise.''

I promised.

''You know I have a little arthritis and I have to do these exercises every day, and now that I'm living with Alan, I do them in the bathroom, with the door closed, so he won't see.''

She sighed with deep feeling.

''Nothing looks so ridiculous as a person doing exercises, especially a large person,'' she said. ''And I don't want to keep reminding Alan of my little ailments. It's nothing serious.''

She grabbed my arm.

''Lydia, you won't believe the trouble I have! You've seen how tiny that bathroom is. When I do this one—'' she started to bend vigorously from side to side, ''I often hit my head on the towel bar. It sticks out at just this height. I told Alan I slipped on the soap the first time, and that the rug skidded the second time. I guess it's silly vanity, but I just don't want him to know that I am in there doing calisthenics. So boring.''

''You poor thing!'' I said. ''Can't you do the exercises when he's out?''

''The doctor said every morning first thing and every night. Alan's always there at those times. What would *you* do, Lydia?''

''Move the towel bar,'' I said.

''Can't very well. It's somehow cemented into

the tile wall. Be a major operation to move it. So expensive."

"Let's have lunch Monday," I said. "I'll try to think of something. Meanwhile, do be careful."

I patted her arm to show that I cared, and we returned to the coffee.

We met on Monday at a little restaurant that we favor because it is almost pitch-dark inside and has an inexpensive lunch special that is quite acceptable. The darkness, especially in the booths, makes it a favorite place for dating couples or women exchanging confidences.

Shirley, her abundant curves bulging in a new outfit, squeezed herself into the booth.

"You won't believe what's happened, Lydia," she said, as we sipped our wine. "I'm so happy I could burst."

I was tempted to say that she certainly looked that way, but that would have been unkind, so I didn't.

"Tell me, tell me!" I said.

"Well, on Saturday morning I was in the bathroom doing my exercises and I heard the most terrible crash. I rushed out, but everything looked normal and then I heard Alan groaning from inside his study. The door was closed, as usual."

She took a sip of wine.

"You know I never go in there if the door is closed. Alan is studying Japanese, in case we take a trip to the Orient, and he has to concentrate without interruption. It's a very difficult language."

"Why don't you study it with him?"

"I'm doing Swedish, in case we go to Scandinavia," she said. "That way we're covered in both directions."

"What a great idea!" I said.

Our lunches arrived. They were substantial sandwiches made with real meat and lettuce, and none of that thready grass purveyed by health food restaurants.

"I opened the study door," Shirley went on, "and there was Alan on the floor, all tangled up under the desk. The chair was overturned, you wouldn't *believe* it, and he was thrashing around, you know how big he is, and trying to get up. Well!"

She shook her head in astonishment at the memory.

"I helped him up and asked him what had happened."

She started to laugh.

"Lydia, you won't *believe* it. He confessed that he was doing exercises for arthritis and somehow tripped over the chair and lost his balance. He said he didn't want me to worry about him or see him doing the exercises because they look so silly."

"Isn't that super!" I said. "Now you can do

them together in the middle of the living room where there's plenty of space."

Shirley looked horrified.

"Oh no," she said. "We'll go on as we are, but we're looking for an apartment with larger rooms. And you must promise not to breathe a word of what I've just told you. Alan wouldn't like it."

"But there's nothing to be ashamed of," I said. "It's not like having, you know, a social disease."

"I know," Shirley said. "What we do, we contribute to the Arthritis Foundation and do our exercises and take our pills and hope that we won't get any worse, and we never *never* talk about it."

She took a bite of her sandwich and chewed it thoughtfully.

"So boring," she said. "Now please tell me what clothes I should take if we go to Sweden. I know you've been there."

When I got home I told Herm that we didn't have to worry any more about Shirley and Alan.

"They are birds of a feather," I said, without going into detail, because I had promised.

"And a credit to the Audubon Society, no doubt," said Herm, who tries to be agreeable even when he isn't quite sure what I am talking about.

8

The Websters' Apartment

"I've just had the most marvelous idea, but you won't like it," I said to Herm one day. He looked slightly apprehensive.

"What is it?"

"I'd like to paint the crawlspace door orange, same as our front door. There's plenty of paint left over."

"I thought the point of having it white, like the house, was to make it inconspicuous," Herm said.

"Yes," I said. "But you can't help seeing it, anyway, as you go up the driveway. And it's ugly."

Everybody has to go up the driveway alongside our house to get to the front door, which is on the rear, because the house is built on a hill going up from the street and the crawlspace is underneath, in front. The crawlspace door is barely five feet high and opens into an unfinished area which is used as a combination attic and toolshed. It holds an accumulation of not-quite-abandoned junk, bags of fertilizer and soil conditioner, half-used cans of paint, and cartons that I save for sending things to the children. Also the hot water heater and water softener. And spiders.

"Hm-m," Herm said.

"What can't be moved might be improved," I said. "Or, to put it another way, roughly, if you can't bear it, repair it."

"Nothing daunted, let's flaunt it," Herm said.

"You're getting the idea."

"It's a pity it's not pretty."

I could tell he was not altogether opposed to my plan.

" 'Twill be less grim with orange trim," Herm said.

"Basta!" I cried. That means Enough! in Spanish, which I was studying in Adult Education.

I hate to paint doors, especially the nasty bits around the doorknob and the hinges, but it looked so bright and happy when it was done that I did not begrudge the labor. While rummaging around for the orange paint I had come across a couple of fancy flower pots that were too garish for indoors and too small for outdoors, but I realized they would be just right for the crawlspace doorway. I filled them with gravel and stuck in some bare branches, to produce what I hoped would be a sort of Oriental effect, and placed one on either side of the door. We had learned from experience that potted plants would not do well on that side of the house.

"Doesn't it look great?" I burbled to Herm, as we stood in the driveway admiring it.

"It's an improvement, all right," Herm said. "Now it looks, almost, as though someone lives there. One of those basement apartments."

It was an intriguing idea. Irresistible, in fact. I inserted a white card into one of those plastic name badge holders, left over from my days of going to PTA meetings (as I keep telling Herm, if you keep something long enough, you will find a use for it, but he doesn't believe me), and tacked it to the door. The card read "A. A. Webster."

"Who the devil is A. A. Webster?" Herm said when he saw it.

"Arachnida Araneida Webster," I said. "She lives there with her family. Araneida is the spider branch of the Arachnid clan."

"Sometimes I wonder about you," he said. "Anyway, no one would believe that's an apartment. There are no windows and the door is too low."

It's true that there are no windows, only a

row of louvered ventilators across the front, and one in the door.

"No one will notice that," I said. "People are not really observant."

"I'll make a bet with you," Herm said. "We'll give it three weeks. If anyone believes that people named Webster actually live there, I'll buy you a new pair of earrings. If, instead, it is pointed out that no one could live in there, you buy me a new rosebush. I'd particularly like Mr. Lincoln."

"You don't have room for another rosebush."

"I'd like to dig up Charlotte Armstrong," Herm said. "I'm tired of her and anyway I want a deeper color. Mr. Lincoln is a good red."

"All right. It's a bet," I said.

The first person to come up the driveway was the water softener man. I had meant to leave a note on the crawlspace door for him, but forgot. He came around to the front door and rang the bell.

"Somebody living down there now?" he asked. "What about the soft water?"

"It's okay," I told him. "It's only the Websters. They won't bother you. Just go right in as usual."

He gave me a funny look before he turned away.

* * *

Herm and I had invited some people over to dinner on Saturday evening of the second week. We had asked the Knights and my friend Poppy and a woman named Laura Bailey whom I had met in my art class. There are never enough men to go around and I have stopped worrying about it. Laura had not been to our house before.

The Knights arrived first. They are a quiet, conventional couple, good-looking and always well-dressed, with whom we share an interest in music. They actually have two grand pianos in their living room, and thump through arrangements of their favorite symphonies and concertos. It is my private suspicion that George always takes the primo part and makes poor Dorothea do the segundo. But it is all right because she adores him. They drove up to the house instead of parking in the street, and I knew it would be a hair-raising experience for them to get their car turned around because there really isn't enough room. They have done it before and missed by two inches taking along a corner of the house when they left. Because they drove up, they didn't notice the orange door.

Poppy arrived next. Since she became a widow she has had little social life, and she came bouncing up the driveway so eager to get to the party that she did not notice the door.

We sat around with our cocktails and I was beginning to wonder what had happened to Laura when the phone rang.

"The strangest thing," Laura said. "I was sure I had found the right house and I parked and walked up the driveway but on the door it said Webster so I came back down again. I'm calling from the gas station at the bottom of the hill. Have you moved?"

"No," I said. "We're right here. I'm sorry. I should have explained about the Websters. Just come up to the back of the house. That's the front."

She made confused noises but said she would be along right away. I told the others what had happened. The Knights, predictably, looked bewildered. Poppy looked worried.

"Isn't that illegal?" she asked.

She tends to be nervous about things, but she can't help it.

Laura came and was introduced. She was wearing a curious garment of an awkward length. It came to mid-calf and appeared to be several bunched-up layers of discarded kitchen curtains, with an all-over print of faded flowers. I took it for a confession of acute poverty but it turned out she had just bought it at the best dress shop in town. She was enchanted by the idea of the Websters, which of course endeared her to me.

Nobody thought it was odd that she had assumed there was an apartment under the house. The others said they would have thought so, too, if they had noticed the door.

I was scoring high.

The next thing that happened was more serious. We received a letter from the city Building Department.

"It has come to our attention," the letter read, "that you have converted the lower portion of your house to a rental unit. However, we have no record of your having applied for a building permit, which is required for all such alterations. Also, this is in violation of the zoning regulations in your neighborhood. In addition, it will be necessary to reassess your house. Please call the building inspector and the assessor for appointments so that they can come and inspect the premises."

Herm was rather angry about it.

"Now look at all the trouble you've caused," he said.

I refrained from saying that he had put the notion of the apartment into my head in the first place, by remarking that it almost looked as though someone lived there.

"What I'd like to know," I said, "is who reported it to the city."

I suspected Mr. Gudge, across the street. He

has been unfriendly ever since we refused to sign his wife's petition. It could not have been the soft water man, because he knew what lay behind the door.

We invited both the building inspector and the assessor to come and look. Herm made a point of being out.

"It's your responsibility," he said. "I'd be embarrassed, trying to explain to them about the Websters."

I thought it would be worth rather a lot just to see the expressions on their faces when I opened the door to the Websters' apartment and ushered them in. And it was.

This afternoon Herm and I are going to the store to select a new pair of earrings. I haven't told him, because I mean it to be a surprise, but I am planning to give him Mr. Lincoln for an un-birthday present. After all, I have won the bet and can afford to be generous.

9

Sparks

When Herm's latest acquisition, the Mr. Lincoln rosebush, bloomed, we gave a small party to celebrate. It was fun for everyone except our friend Poppy, who stood around looking so wistful it almost broke my heart. Poppy is a widow who has never adjusted to the solitary life. I used to tell her, at least once a week, to take up bird-watching, or carpentry, or television repair, but she would say that she just wasn't really excited about birds, or hammering. As though that mattered. So after a while I decided to stop telling her. It is my considered opinion that a lot of unhappiness is self-imposed. Sometimes I think Poppy enjoys unhappiness just as some people enjoy their physical ailments. It gives them something interesting to brood about.

"How can you expect to find a man," I asked her, "if you don't go to where the men are?"

"Oh Lydia," she said. "You're such a do-it-yourselfer. I expect the man to find *me*."

"My grandmother used to say 'God helps those who help themselves,' " I said.

It was like talking to the wall.

I know lots of widows who, once they recovered from the shock of losing their husbands, found themselves having more fun than they ever had before. Poppy simply felt lost and helpless.

I invited her to go with me one evening to a recital of contemporary chamber music. Herm looked so pained when I suggested that he go that I hastily backed off and told him that I was sure Poppy would really *like* to go. In actual fact, Poppy finds contemporary music as hard to take as Herm does, but she is always so glad to be invited to go anywhere that she accepted immediately.

In the car the same old subject came up.

"If you had a nice man to cuddle at home," I said, "you wouldn't be here now on your way to a recital that you won't like. Of course, that would be hard on *me*, but I'd rather see you happy."

"Maybe the music won't be so bad this time," Poppy said.

"If you are just waiting for Mr. Perfect to come along and find you, you'll probably have a long wait. Like the rest of your life."

I can't help it. I have an unshakable conviction that if you keep pounding on something, it will eventually give way.

Poppy said, "Suppose I went to some of those places you suggested and suppose I met a man who was suitable, what if there weren't any sparks between us? It's no use, Lydia. All the men I've seen look so old and I can't imagine sparks flying at all."

I was so astonished by this that I nearly ran a red light.

"Sparks!" I said. "Sparks! You want the moon with maple syrup on it."

"Well, but—"

"If you find just one decent man," I said, "who shows any interest in you, you'd better grab him fast, because if you don't, there are plenty of other eager women who'll get there ahead of you. While you are still looking for the sparks."

"I'm sure you're right," Poppy said, "but it sounds so cold-blooded."

"It's not really cold-blooded, just sensible," I said.

We had arrived at the concert hall and the subject was dropped. The music, if it could be called that, consisted of beeping noises from a machine on a table, rasping noises from a pot scrubber drawn across a sheet of metal, and occasional slaps and twangs on cellos played by three persons who from time to time lifted their heads and ululated. I was thankful that Herm wasn't there. He would have stalked out right in the middle of a piece called "Sounds Rising and Falling," and since the audience consisted almost entirely of students, I knew that we— because of course I would have had to stalk out with him, to show my loyalty—would have been branded, contemptuously, as old fogies. Nevertheless, I was glad when it was over and we could go home.

Poppy called me a week later.

"There's a new adult ed class that I think would help me," she said. "I wondered if you'd go with me. I'm a little uneasy about going alone."

"What's it about?" I said.

"It's called 'Let It Out' and it says here 'Share Your Problems and Learn to Solve Them.' It's in the afternoon, so it wouldn't interfere with your painting."

I agreed to go, out of curiosity as much as friendship. Poppy said she would meet me there.

In the classroom, the chairs were arranged in a semicircle facing the desk. About twenty people, ranging in age from eighteen to eighty, straggled in out of the rain and took places. I saved a seat for Poppy, who arrived in a snappy red outfit with exactly matching lipstick.

I looked around at the others and realized that I had never before been in such dreary company. They were the people who couldn't cope and were here seeking help. I hoped they would find it, they all seemed so pitiful.

The instructor arrived, deposited a tape recorder and a bundle of papers on the desk, and wrote her name on the blackboard, Mrs. Vashti O'Connor. She was an attractive woman of about forty, wearing a brilliantly colored caftan under her raincoat. She passed around an attendance sheet for us to sign, and said, "We all have problems, but by sharing them we can help each other and progress toward inner peace. I am going to play you some rhythmic Indian music to set the mood."

She turned on the tape recorder and through the static we could hear faint drumming. I decided that Mrs. O'Connor was a phony but she might do a bit of good anyway.

There was some nervous foot-shuffling among the students, resulting in a few wet umbrellas being kicked around, but otherwise everyone was, presumably, getting into the mood.

After a few minutes Mrs. O'Connor switched off the recorder.

"Now," she said, "who will start by telling us about his or her problem?"

That made two strikes against Mrs. O'Connor. I find this "his or her" business awkward and unnecessary, and feel that the militant women who insist on it are straining at gnats.

No one volunteered. I sneaked a sideways glance at Poppy. She appeared to be spellbound.

Mrs. O'Connor said, "Well then, we'll just start here at the end and go along."

She looked expectantly at the student in the first seat on her right. It was a woman with what appeared to be a bundle of scarves around her neck, as though she had forgotten she had one on, and added another, and then another. I supposed it was her interpretation of what is called the layered look.

"My problem is my children," she said. And she went on to explain that she had to work and the children were getting out of hand.

Mrs. O'Connor asked the class for suggestions. The prospects of anyone coming up with a helpful thought were dim, but probably just giving voice to the difficulty was therapeutic.

I was sorry for the scarf woman, especially because I felt she was wasting her time in Mrs. O'Connor's class and would be better off if she went home and either spanked or hugged her children. But of course I couldn't say that.

There was a moment of uncomfortable silence. Then Mrs. O'Connor said, "Well, let's all think about this and be ready next week with some good advice."

She turned to the next student, a man with a sad, lined face. He shook his head and said, "I'd rather wait a little."

Mrs. O'Connor assumed an indulgent expression and said, "All right, we'll skip you for now."

Next in line was a stout middle-aged woman who had a mother-in-law problem. She went on at length, becoming rather heated about it, so that I fancied I actually saw steam rising from her raincoat. Mrs. O'Connor had to stop her, finally, because it was getting late.

"We'll all think about these problems for next week," she said, "and I want you each to bring a bag of sand and one of those aluminum foil roasting pans."

So far as I was concerned, Mrs. O'Connor had struck out. I said as much to Poppy when we emerged into the rain. She had been fumbling with her umbrella, but she finally got it open and said, "I'm not sure about coming back, myself, Lydia. I have a feeling that they're going to start talking about sex."

"That would be more fun than today," I said. "You wouldn't want to miss it."

Poppy was not convinced that the class would do her any good, but, she told me, Mrs. O'Connor was the sister of a woman she knew in the Ladies' Choral Society and she didn't want to hurt anyone's feelings by dropping out so soon. The upshot was that she went alone to the next session and called me afterward.

"You wanted to know what the sand was for," she reminded me. "Well, we had to pour it into the pans we brought, and take off our shoes and put our feet in it."

"Heaven help us!" I said.

"Mrs. O'Connor said it would relax us and help us to communicate."

"Did it?"

"Not everybody brought sand. You remember that man who wouldn't talk?"

"Yes," I said.

"His name is Wilfred and his problem is that his wife died a couple of years ago and he . . . uh . . . well, he can't get used to it."

"Yes," I said again. "He looked like a nice man. And lonesome."

"Honestly, Lydia!" Poppy said. "Anyway, he's quite old."

"Um," I said.

I don't think Poppy realizes that she is no

spring chicken herself. Also, although she is a bit younger, she looks older than I do. At least Herm assures me this is the case.

"Honestly, Lydia!" Poppy said again, and hung up.

The Choral Society was rehearsing for a performance, so Poppy was kept busy and I didn't see her, but a week later she called me again.

"I was talking to Wilfred, you know in the class, and he invited me to go for a walk and a picnic lunch in the park day after tomorrow. Do you think that's all right?"

She sounded quite excited.

"I think it's marvelous," I said. "I hope you offered to bring the fried chicken, or whatever."

"I don't want to lead him on," Poppy said, "because I don't think I could be romantically interested in him. But of course it's nice to have a man friend."

"Maybe all he wants is someone to picnic with," I said. "In that case, I wish you both a happy day."

Between the Choral Society rehearsals and picnicking with Wilfred, Poppy had little time for anything else. When I met her one day in the supermarket, buying paper plates, she told me that she and Wilfred had both dropped out of Mrs. O'Connor's class and were spending their time in the park instead.

"I thought the other day," Poppy said, "but of course I couldn't be sure, but I thought that maybe there might be just the beginning of a little spark. You know?"

"Fan it gently and be careful not to blow it out," I said. "One nice thing about Los Barcos, you can picnic even in the winter."

I doubt that the scarf woman ever received much help with her problem, and I know that mothers-in-law are either loved or hated, there can be no in-between, but for at least two of her students, Mrs. O'Connor's class was a great success. I think I owe her an apology.

10

Yielding Is Sin

"Why is it," I said to Herm one day as we drove downtown, "that if I only so much as look at a piece of pie or a chocolate éclair, I gain weight? It's like those people who get a rash from just walking past the poison ivy, but there's a scientific basis for *that*. Particles of venom in the air."

"I don't believe it's called venom," said Herm, who as usual had been only half listening.

It's true that I do my most serious thinking while driving, and often think out loud, so I don't expect Herm to pay attention. In fact, I prefer that he doesn't. But when I do address him, he is not always aware of it. Of course, it is possible that he is involved in some serious thinking of his own.

We were on our way to do some errands, one of which was to stop at Monty's Art Supplies so that I could pick up a tube of Prussian blue. There is a city parking lot right behind Monty's but no back door into the shop, so that one has to walk out to a side street and around the corner to get to Monty's front door, or take a shortcut through a passage which used to provide access to the drive-in window of a shoe repair establishment next door to Monty's. Although it would have been convenient to take our shoes there, we never did, because we were put off by a sign which read: NO Work Done While U Wait! There was something offensive about the large black letters of the word "NO." Other people must have found the sign offensive, too, because the shop went out of business, and remodeling for something new was started.

Herm elected to wait for me in the car. He likes to use snippets of time like that to catch up on his reading, and keeps a supply of magazines behind the seat. At home he can seldom find time to read because he is usually working in the garden.

The shortcut passage was at last clear of workmen's debris, the passage window of the erstwhile shoe repair shop was open, and from it issued a smell, a fragrance, an aroma, a perfume more enticing than Chanel Number Five, more spellbinding than magic, a smell guaranteed to weaken the resolve of the staunchest, to lure the hapless passerby into utmost danger, a veritable siren song of a smell, the smell of baking. When I reached the street, I found the shop door invitingly open, and a sign in the window proclaimed that Aunt Emily's Cakes and Cookies were available within.

I went on to Monty's, bought the Prussian blue, tried to pass Aunt Emily's open door on my way back to the passage, but was sucked inside like a crumb into a vacuum cleaner. Two sparkling display counters had replaced the grimy appointments of the shoe repair shop, the floor was softly pink and white, and the walls papered with a design of rosebuds. Behind the rear counter stood a tall girl with dark hair and a large, firm chin. She looked like a weight lifter.

I inspected the merchandise, laid out on trays under the glass. It looked as good as it smelled. The rear showcase held cakes of every description, and the one along the side was full of cookies, not measly little wafers or health food horrors full of oats and bran and fit only for horses, but beautiful creations in a variety of shapes, crescents, ovals, spirals, some lusciously frosted with chocolate, some swirled with lemon or vanilla ribbons, some like thin flaky sandwiches stuffed with whipped-cream filling, inviting you to lick off the edges before taking a bite.

"Is there really an Aunt Emily back there doing all this?" I asked the girl.

"Oh yes," she said, smiling faintly. "I am Aunt Emily."

"Oh. Well, everything looks very nice. Tell me, what are these?"

I pointed to some rectangular objects of delicately molded pastry, with ridged tops studded with almonds.

"Bear claws," said Aunt Emily.

"What took you so long?" Herm asked when I finally returned to the car.

"I was buying you a present," I said, handing him the tiny white bag containing a bear claw.

He pretended to be shocked but was, of course, pleased. We broke the bear claw in half and shared it, sitting in the car and getting crumbs all over everything. To say that it was delicious would be an understatement.

A few days later I found that I needed a new number 7 brush. Again I was sucked into Aunt Emily's on my way back to the car, and handed Herm a bag with two flat round cinnamon crisps. They were even more delicious than the bear claw.

On the third occasion, when I had to have a new pencil before I could start the sketch assigned for the next art class, Herm, eager to finish a magazine that he had tossed into my car, accompanied me as usual. We had no sooner left the driveway and started down the street than he began to sing, in a slow pontifical manner.

> Yield not to temp-ta-tion,
> For yield-ing is sin,
> Each vic-t'ry will help you
> Some oth-er to win.

He was gazing out the window and acting as though he did not even know I was there.

> Fight man-ful-ly on-ward,
> Dark pas-sions sub-due, . . .

"Enough!" I said. "I get the message."

After parking the car, instead of going through the passage to Monty's, I went out to the side street and walked around the corner, altogether avoiding Aunt Emily. It took longer, but I was able to return to the car feeling smugly virtuous. Was it my imagination, or did Herm look ever so slightly disappointed when I appeared, carrying only a new pencil? Nothing was said, however, and we did the rest of our errands and went home, just as though Aunt Emily did not exist.

"I need another tube of titanium white," I

said to Herm the next day. "It seems to get used up awfully fast."

He looked at me suspiciously.

"I'll just come along, if you don't mind," he said. "It will give me a chance to finish that article I started yesterday."

Knowing that Herm was watching, I left the parking lot ostentatiously by the exit leading to the side street, and arrived at Monty's without having to pass Aunt Emily's. On the way out, however, a little devil whispered in my ear that it wouldn't hurt just to peek in the window for a minute. That, of course, was my undoing.

Never before had I deceived Herm, but Aunt Emily, with her jutting chin, was too strong for me. I stood furtively against the wall in the passage and gobbled half a French waffle, stowing away the remaining half, carefully wrapped, at the bottom of my handbag, to be finished later in the privacy of my studio. I inspected my face for crumbs, sprayed my mouth with peppermint, like an alcoholic, and, hoping that I did not look as guilty as I felt, returned to the parking lot by the longer roundabout route, flourishing my tube of paint.

It was the beginning of what was later referred to as Lydia's Downfall. Pangs of conscience and fear of discovery made me realize that the life of a wrongdoer, whatever its gratifications, is one of uneasiness and anxiety. But I had become an addict. Herm pointed out that, with only a little advance planning, I could cut down considerably on the number of trips to Monty's. I was kept busy thinking of emergency reasons for going there.

Then a new problem arose. It was one I had foreseen and dreaded. One morning I was able to zip into my favorite slacks only with difficulty. It was a bad moment. Any day now Herm would finish studying the new seed catalogs and begin to notice me again. It was time for desperate measures. Cold turkey.

I consulted the Yellow Pages, studied the list of artists' supply shops, and decided on one connected with a paint and wallpaper store in a section of town given over mostly to thrift shops and seedy hotels. It was an area I usually avoided. In that utterly dismal neighborhood there would be no Aunt Emily lurking with hypnotic powers and little pink cakes.

"Now you're getting smart," Herm commented, when I emerged from the paint store with enough supplies for several weeks. "But why not get it at Monty's?"

"It's cheaper here," I said, hoping this was true.

He gave me one of those penetrating looks he

usually reserves for his rosebushes when he suspects the presence of enemy bugs.

"I think you are running away from Aunt Emily," he said.

"And what if I am?"

"You should never run away from a problem," Herm said. "Be strong. Stay and face it."

There are times when even a good man can be hateful. But I have learned what to do in such a situation. Nothing. Above all, maintain a dignified silence. So I did.

Every month or so we went downtown to the paint store to replenish my supplies. One day, however, I needed a tube of ivory black and the paint store was all out of it.

"Let's go to Monty's," Herm said. "I'll go in with you and keep you out of trouble."

We parked in the lot behind Monty's and walked through the passage. Heavenly smells came through Aunt Emily's window.

"Just this once," I begged.

Herm relented. Actually, I think he was as overpowered by the smell as I was.

Aunt Emily stood behind the rear counter. We bought a bear claw to share.

"I haven't seen you for a while," Aunt Emily said, making change. "I suppose you've been away."

"Uh . . . yes. How's business?"

"The fact is," Aunt Emily said, "business has been so good for the wedding and birthday cakes that I am closing the shop and going into custom baking, which I can do from my own home."

She handed me the tiny white bag.

"It's more profitable than making all these little things, and I won't have to rent a shop."

"We'll miss you," I said. "But good luck to you."

It was pleasant to be able to go to Monty's again without experiencing temptation and guilt. A barber has set up his business in the former bakery. Nothing of interest there.

Herm has a birthday coming up pretty soon and I have decided to order a cake from Aunt Emily. It will have a chocolate frosting and in white letters the message "Yielding is sin." Aunt Emily won't understand what it is all about but Herm will. It will be my revenge for all the suffering I endured.

11

Our Friend Snowfoot

I believe that everyone is entitled to a few harmless eccentricities. In fact, without them we all would be as undistinguished as pancakes, faceless and identical. So when I discovered, on our daily walks, that Herm often feels prompted to make noises at animals, I never try to stop him.

Herm makes no attempt to produce authentic sounds. If a noisy crow flies overhead, Herm will look up at it and shout "Caw caw caw," even if there are other people around. When a dog behind a fence barks fiercely, causing me to jump in fright, Herm always pauses and calls out "Orf! Orf!" "Orf" does not sound much like a dog sound, but "Orf" is what Herm says. Some dogs are so astonished that they stop barking immediately. Others are driven into a frenzy of excitement.

It is with cats, however, that Herm really scores. He used to have a couple of Siamese, long before we ever met, and although we have no room in our present lives for domestic animals, he retains a soft spot for them. Whenever we pass a cat sitting on its doorstep or nosing around its garden, Herm can't resist. "Kitty kitty," he says. "Nice kitty." Invariably the cat comes over and rubs against our legs. Herm scratches its head. A good time is had by both. Sometimes the cat will even accompany us to the corner.

One day I found Herm out on the balcony calling "Meow meow." In the garden the Gudges' cat, Snowfoot, from across the street, was attacking a boulder, trying to dig out lizards. Snowfoot is black with white feet. He is a mighty hunter.

"Kitty kitty," Herm said seductively.

Snowfoot turned and replied politely, then resumed digging.

It all seemed quite innocent and I paid no further attention. We like the lizards but did not think it likely that Snowfoot would catch them.

One day, however, I heard agitated bird calls from the wild part of the garden and peered out of the kitchen door to see what was happening. I surprised Snowfoot hurrying away with a bird in his mouth. I couldn't bear to look closely but prayed that it was one of the overabundant finches and not our resident wrentit. When it comes to birds, I am a snob.

Whereas I had formerly tolerated Snowfoot's presence, this incident made me see him in a different light. I took to shooing him away, clapping my hands and shouting "Scat!" whenever he appeared. The trouble was that Snowfoot was so convinced that we were his friends that he didn't understand my changed attitude. Herm said it was useless to worry about it because there was no way to keep Snowfoot from trespassing. He was right, of course, but he did stop talking to Snowfoot, to show his disapproval. This is where matters stood on the date of my coffee party.

For some years I have kept up my membership in a club called the Happy Girls. It is so named because the members are lonely females who have moved here for one reason or another, leaving behind all their friends and relations. Happy Girls has scouts who find these people and invite them to join the club, where they make new friends and engage in a variety of decorous activities, something for every taste. After a while, many of the members drift off into other pursuits but continue to meet occasionally so as not to lose touch with the Happy Girls who first befriended them. My involvement with them is now limited to attending a coffee from time to time, and now it was my turn to be the hostess.

My friend Poppy, whom I had first met in the Happy Girls, offered to be assistant hostess, which meant that she would bring some cookies and help to answer the door when the guests arrived. I made her promise not to bring one of those horrible cakes she likes to make, full of gelatin and imitation whipped cream and maraschino cherries. She was disappointed.

Herm cut some of his best roses for me to use on the table, and announced that he would be leaving.

"I'll be back in time for lunch," he told me, stressing the word "lunch." "Try to save a cookie for me."

The Happy Girls were due to arrive at ten-thirty but Poppy said she would come at ten to help me with last-minute preparations. She arrived promptly, ringing the door bell with such force that I knew something was wrong.

When I opened the door she was standing there, pale and shaking. I took the pan from her hands before she dropped it.

"Poppy! What's the matter?"

She staggered into the house.

"Close the door," she said. "And put down the pan."

I complied.

"And now call Herm."

"I can't. He's gone for the morning."

"Oh no! Look outside. What are we going to do?"

I opened the door and looked. In the carport Snowfoot sat on top of my car, washing his face. When he saw me, he stopped washing and began to purr. He had brought us a present, as cats sometimes do.

The present, a dead hedge rat, lay on the ground in front of the doormat. Snowfoot had eaten part of it and brought the rest to share with us. There was a fair amount of blood around. I hastily closed the door.

"We've got to do something before the Girls come," Poppy said.

The obvious thing to do was get a shovel, bury the rat, and wash away the traces, but neither of us had the fortitude for that.

"Here, Poppy," I said, handing back her pan of cookies. "You set these out and look after things in the kitchen. I'll do something."

I clenched my teeth and went to the toolshed where Herm kept some extra flowerpots. There was a five-gallon plastic pot that would do. I clapped it upside down over the rat, while Snowfoot watched with interest. But if he decided to have another snack, I knew he could easily push it away. I weighted it down with a potted azalea and hoped for the best.

"Scat!" I shouted at Snowfoot. "Go home!"

Snowfoot yawned and continued to wash his face.

It was no use. I returned to the kitchen where Poppy was arranging her cookies on a platter. She had found a new recipe, she told me happily. It was called Carob Peanut Marvels and combined carob powder, peanut butter, pineapple, and egg whites, which made it very healthful. She had decorated them with the maraschino cherries she had bought before I put thumbs down on the gelatin cake. I reminded myself that Poppy was, at heart, a good woman and anyway, everyone should be allowed a few harmless eccentricities.

The Happy Girls arrived. Poppy stood outside to greet them, steering them carefully around the azalea, which stood exactly where they might trip over it. The party was a success, with lots of gossip. No one spilled coffee on the carpet. But although twenty Happy Girls had crowded around the table, only two Carob Peanut Marvels had been eaten by the time they left. I was glad I had set out some Lemon Fingers and pound cake, all of which had disappeared.

Poppy eyed the platter with dismay.

"You'll take some of them, won't you, Lydia?" she said.

"Herm would be thrilled," I said. "He specially asked me to save him a cookie."

Poppy took half of them home, which left seventeen for Herm.

When I heard his car in the driveway I went out to meet him. Snowfoot was not in sight.

"What's this?" Herm said, when he saw the azalea.

"Snowfoot brought you a present," I said. "I'll get lunch ready while you take care of it."

"Well," he said, in a false hearty voice when he came in, "it's really great, isn't it, to have Snowfoot around. We won't have to worry about rodents in the garden."

I said nothing.

"Did the Happy Girls see it?"

"No," I said. "It's all your fault, Herm. For making friends with that cat. I've had a horrible morning and I'm sure Poppy will have nightmares for a week."

"Snowfoot really *is* our friend, Lydia. But, well, I'm sorry."

"This is your punishment," I said, and produced the plate of Carob Peanut Marvels.

Herm looked at them and recoiled.

"That's unconstitutional," he said. "Article VIII

of the Bill of Rights forbids the infliction of cruel and unusual punishments.''

"I suppose you're right," I said. "Perhaps we should give them to Snowfoot."

But that would have been cruelty to animals. So I threw them out.

After lunch we went for our daily walk. We chose a street with some interesting gardens, and as we passed a fine eugenia hedge, a dog on the other side began to bark at us.

"Orf! Orf!" Herm responded, taking my hand so that I wouldn't be frightened.

"Orf!" I chimed in, just to let Herm know that I think he is really a very sweet guy.

12

The Fashion of This World

Everything began to go wrong the day I read a magazine article that urged women to avoid looking middle-aged and matronly by keeping up with fashion and not continuing to dress as they had done ten or twenty years earlier. You can be the Ageless Woman rather than the Aging Frump, the article said. There were photographs of an Aging Frump, with her blouse hanging loosely four inches below her cardigan, and a smartly dressed Ageless Woman, obviously setting out for her job as a top executive. I was impressed.

"Herm," I said, "I have decided to be an Ageless Woman."

"That's fine, Sugar," Herm said, looking up from his garden catalog. "I think I'll try some early peas this year."

I dashed downtown, bought a pattern and

some fabric for one of those slipslop dresses that are so fashionable now, and retired to my sewing corner. The dress had a tie at the neck and a ruffle at the bottom. In between it had the shape of a grocery bag. Before hemming it, I tried it on.

In the fashion pictures the tie is always left undone, the ends dangling, and one shoulder of the garment about to slide off. Perhaps this is supposed to look sexy, but to me it just looks slovenly. I tied mine in a neat bow. The ruffle at the bottom was at odds with my sneakers, so I changed to shoes with heels.

Herm came in as I was posing before the mirror. He gave me a critical once-over and shook his head.

"No," he said. "It's not right for you. You have to be willowy to wear a thing like that and you're not willowy."

I looked in the mirror and saw a fat wrinkled hag in an ugly dress.

"Okay," I said. "I'll give it to the thrift shop. Maybe some poor but willowy person will buy it."

Anyway, making it had helped take my mind off the fact that I had not heard from Julie, my daughter, for several weeks and was getting worried. Maybe one of the children was sick. If I telephoned they would think I was fussing.

I put the dress into a carton already full of items for the thrift shop, and invited Herm to ride downtown with me.

We took the route that goes past the high school, unaware, until too late, that it was the time in the afternoon when school lets out and hordes of teenagers are milling around. The car ahead of us, driven by a high school girl, stopped suddenly in the middle of the street. I braked. In the car behind us an angry man stuck his head out of the window. A teenage boy sauntered over to the girl's car, leaned on the door frame, and began to chat with her. I honked. He glanced back at us, laughed, and returned to his chat. I leaned out and said, "If you want to talk, pull over to the side." The boy laughed again. The man behind us was backing up, preparing to pull around. I could feel my temper rising. I honked again. The boy turned. "Why don't you stay on the freeway, if you're in such a hurry," he said.

The angry man had pulled out and I backed up and followed suit. I considered taking the girl's license number but knew it would be useless. The police would be unable and unwilling to do anything.

"Don't let it get to you, Lydia," Herm said. "Let's just not go on this street any more."

"It's the last straw," I said. "I wasted my time

on that horrible dress and I'm worried about the children and you said I was too fat and now that insolent punk—"

"I never said you were too fat," Herm said.

That was Wednesday. The kind of day I wouldn't wish on anybody. The kind of day that would not happen to the indomitable Ageless Woman in the magazine picture.

Our Thursday morning routine is always the same. I stuff my purse full of newspaper coupons, find my shopping list, and say to Herm, "I'll be off now to do the marketing. Would you like to come?"

"I had planned to do some weeding this morning, but I'll be glad to come if you need me," Herm says.

The first part of this statement is obviously untrue, as Herm is already dressed in his supermarket outfit, which is somewhat more formal than his gardening clothes. But this is part of our Thursday ritual.

At the market, Herm takes charge of pushing the cart and lifting the bags in and out of the car afterward. The trouble is, I keep losing him. I take down four or five cans of tomatoes, on sale that week, turn to deposit them in the cart, and find that it is nowhere in sight. Herm has it parked two aisles over, where he is inspecting imported delicacies that we would never dream of buying. It is particularly frustrating to have the cart vanish when I am juggling two clammy cartons of milk.

Sometimes I wish I could explain to Herm that I am really quite strong and not in need of assistance.

On the Thursday after that terrible Wednesday, we started out as usual. In the detergent aisle we encountered Mr. and Mrs. Frobish, who seem much older than they really are because, now that they are retired, their minds and bodies have become atrophied, not from disease but from disuse. In the watery soup of their lives, daily expeditions to the supermarket and the drugstore provide the only scraps of social nourishment. They were squabbling mildly about what size box of Happiwash to buy. We greeted them and hurried on, feeling guilty because we did not stop for conversation. But they are so dull.

I started down the canned goods aisle, although I saw that Herm had been sidetracked into Health Foods, which I refuse to have in the house. My contention is that most foods are healthful if properly prepared in a kitchen and not in a factory. Then it occurred to me that the kind of people who wear slipslop dresses eat mostly alfalfa sprouts, yogurt, and granola. Come to think of it, maybe that is why they are willowy.

I wondered what an Ageless Woman eats. Nothing was said about it in the article.

This depressing train of thought was broken abruptly by a four-year-old boy who careered into me, heading for the candy counter at the end of the aisle, and causing me to drop a can of grapefruit juice on my foot. The child's mother stood at the beginning of the aisle with her cart, loaded with groceries and a baby about nine months old. She was a dark-haired young woman with a harassed expression and a slipslop dress that looked even worse than mine. As I turned to pick up the can of juice, she took a deep breath and yelled, "MANFRED J. MERGELKAMP, come back here THIS MINUTE!"

The little boy had climbed up on the candy shelf to reach the chocolate bars at the top, and now, with two of them firmly in his grasp, he darted away. From the look on Mrs. Mergelkamp's face I foresaw trouble for Manfred when she caught up with him. Well, maybe it's not so great to be young, I thought. Young or old, you can't win.

Herm appeared. He always gets a cart that goes sideways. It is fate and must be accepted.

"I think all the prices have gone up since last week," he said.

I waited for what I knew was coming next.

"I can remember when lemons were two cents apiece," Herm said.

"Well, I can't," I said. "Let's go home."

A howl from the next aisle announced that Mrs. Mergelkamp had found Manfred.

At the checkout counter Herm picked up a sensational tabloid and I leafed through a housewife magazine, turning to the recipes because I had had it with high fashion. My eye was caught by a glorious full-color picture that looked as though it should be entitled Fat Lady's Party Treat, but was actually Sweet 'n' Sauer Salad Secret. It was made with sauerkraut, chopped onion tops, and pimientos molded into a lemon gelatin dessert mix and topped by a dollop of mayonnaise laced with horseradish. After reading about this, I was not surprised to notice that the front page of Herm's tabloid predicted the imminent end of the world.

If the prediction turned out to be correct, it wouldn't make any difference if I were an Ageless Woman or not.

I returned the magazine to the rack and tried giving the evil eye to a woman up ahead who had written a check for $1.31 but had no credentials, so that the manager had to be summoned and there was rather a foofaraw before she left.

On the way home I thought about an article I had read some years ago by an English writer,

Katherine Whitehorn. She advised that when a day starts off badly, there is no point in trying to improve it. She said that the smart thing is to use the day to good advantage by doing all the odd nasty jobs that you keep putting off because they *are* nasty, but which have to be done sometime soon. The day is ruined anyway. I condensed the whole thing into a few words, to wit: You can't change a fiasco into a fiesta.

She did not say what to do if there are several bad days in a row.

I decided to spend the rest of Thursday cleaning the stove. Herm doesn't like it when I clean the stove because afterward, reluctant to get it dirty again, I tend to serve cold meals for a week or so.

Herm was in the garden and I was drearily scouring a burner pan when the mailman came. He brought the usual bundle of junk mail. Mixed in with it was a letter from the children. The letter was three weeks old because they kept forgetting to buy stamps, they said.

It dawned on me, in a flash of insight, that slipslop dresses were just a temporary fad and that state of mind was more important than costume in one's progress toward being an Ageless Woman.

I put away the cleaning equipment and went out to the garden.

Herm, as usual, was puttering with his roses. He looked up.

"You know what, Lydia? I just remembered what Paul said about fashion."

"Paul who?" I said.

"St. Paul. In the first Epistle to the Corinthians. He said, 'The fashion of this world passeth away.'"

"He was absolutely right," I said.

13

The Fund

Almost every day Herm and I drive to some part of town, park the car, and enjoy a brisk two-mile walk. Herm, ever the naturalist, examines the shrubs in the gardens we pass. I like to look at the houses. Sometimes we walk in parks. It is pleasant as well as invigorating.

The other day, on the way home from one of these excursions, we stopped at a vegetable market run by the Seekers of Glorious Light. They are young people who engage in communal living and organic farming somewhere outside of town. They are all, especially the girls, excessively hairy. It may be part of their philosophy to shun the razor. But their vegetables are good and often cheaper than the ones at the supermarket. I left Herm in the car and dashed in to pick up a head of lettuce and some garlic.

As I was checking out, with two lettuces, garlic, broccoli, mushrooms, baby squashes, a bag of apples, and some cheese, the checker I call Gorilla Girl looked at me with the interest and respect accorded to a historical marker along the highway, and said, "I want to let you know. We are telling all our elderly customers that they are eligible for a ten percent discount."

I hope this gentle creature will never realize the enormity of her deed. But I am proud to report that I rose to the occasion. Looking her right in the eye, I said with perfect aplomb, "Thank you. I'll tell my mother."

Thank goodness Herm had stayed in the car. I shall never tell him of this. But more was to come.

That same evening we attended a free chamber music recital at the local college. The audience for the free recitals is mostly students and we find the atmosphere heady. Sometimes a busload of senior citizens from Casa Hermosa or some other local retirement home will turn up. They, too, enjoy free entertainment. They file in neatly and all sit together, a couple of rows of white, gray, and bald heads. When Herm and I, in a jolly mood, accepted our programs from the usher in her faded bedspread dress, she, eager to be of assistance, said, "Are you with the group from Casa Hermosa?"

Thud! There went the evening.

We sat as far as possible from the Casa Hermosa gang, absently noting that we were the only people in our row with shoes on, and during a rather dull string quartet I tried to face the truth. Lydia, I said to myself, you are no longer a person. You are, at least in the eyes of others, a senior citizen, although you are not yet eligible for Social Security, free bus tickets, or reduced rates at movies you wouldn't go to see even if they were free. That settles it. I shall have to be more serious about my Fund.

Yes, I have this little savings account, to which I add a bit now and then, hoping eventually to build it up to enough for a face-lift. But every year something more urgent and exciting, like an impulsive trip abroad, depletes it. Herm knows nothing of this. He is content with his wrinkles and white hair, and finds it very comfortable to be an "elderly customer." I wish *he* had gone in to get that lettuce. He thinks face-lifting is stupid. "Destroys the expression," he says. "Woman looks like a zombie." That is why I keep dipping into my Fund. So long as Herm has that attitude, there is no pressure about being dewrinkled. Until now.

Disasters happen in threes, of course.

The next day Herm's granddaughter Sandra, fifteen, called to ask if she could stop in after school with a couple of friends, to look at my pictures. I was very flattered and had to take extra care not to twitter. When they arrived, Sandra explained that her friend, Summer Dawn, was interested in painting and planned to go to the Art Institute after graduating from high school. Summer Dawn, despite her poetic name, did not strike me as an artistic type, but you never know. Before going to the studio, I offered them lemonade and cookies.

They perched on the sofa, like three bedraggled birds on a wire, their tattered jeans and T-shirts incongruous in my civilized living room: Sandra, Summer Dawn, and the third one whose name I never did get. They were sweet, naive, and a bit shy. I decided to paint them, later, from memory. They kept eating cookies and began to talk about one of their teachers, known to them as The Flab, whom they disliked intensely.

"What a revolting nickname!" I said, but carefully, smiling.

"Oh, Lydia," Sandra said. "If you could see her! She's always writing things on the board. She lifts her arm, like this, and writes stuff, and all that—ugh, flab!—just wobbles. It makes us feel sick. Honestly."

"It's too, you know, gross," said Summer Dawn.

"Oh man, you know," said the third one.

I tried to sound cool and sensible.

"That has nothing to do with how good a teacher she is."

"But, Lydia, we can't bear to look at her," said Sandra.

"She should wear long sleeves, that would take care of it," I said, composedly stroking my own.

But they were not convinced. Even if The Flab should now come to school decently covered, it would be too late. They have seen what is underneath and would never forget it.

I had planned, after the girls' visit, to go to a new shop that sells jewelry made of some kind of puttylike stuff that never really hardens, so you can squeeze it into different shapes as the fancy takes you, but that seemed, suddenly, unsuitable. Why bother to hang ornaments on a withered crone? Instead, I decided to pop down to the bank and add a few dollars to my Fund.

On the way to the bank, thinking hard as I always do when I drive, I realized with a jolt that even if I had my face lifted and wore flab-concealing clothes, Gorilla Girl, the bedspread-dress girl, and all their contemporaries would still identify me as one of the Casa Hermosa group, entitled to a discount. You can't fool them. I changed direction and headed for the putty jewelry. If I am lucky, I thought, they will have some in a color to go with my new jumpsuit.

14

Contact

Herm and I were having dinner at our favorite neighborhood bistro, a dimly lit place with plastic tablecloths, run by a Mexican family. The food is good, if you like Mexican food, which we do.

We were polishing off our enchiladas when Herm's attention was diverted from his plate and fixed upon my streaming face.

"Lydia," he said, "I'm sure that anything that makes your eyes water like that will eat holes in your stomach."

It is true that I have a passion for salsa, otherwise known as hot sauce, and use it liberally. But salsa was not the cause of my tears. I was breaking in a pair of contact lenses. One of them slipped out and fell on my plate. I fished it out, dripping with salsa, wrapped it in a napkin, and put it in my handbag.

I have read that a fashion cycle runs its course in six years, from introduction through popularity to decline. It is usually in the last stages of decline, just before its demise, that I become reconciled to it and take it up. The result is that my wardrobe is always out of date and I feel dowdy. Fortunately, Herm is completely oblivious to such things, although he is no slouch at spotting what he calls "a good-looking older girl."

Anyway, during the years when everyone had contact lenses and myopia was as carefully concealed as a social disease, I plodded along with my old plastic frames openly perched on my nose, and just when it became the In thing to hide behind racing driver goggles, I finally decided to take up contacts.

Everything seemed to be going as well as could be expected. The thrill of being transformed from an ugly duckling to a glamour girl (at least, that was how I felt about it) was ample compensation for the eye irritation that caused me to go about with a perpetual grimace. I never suspected that the squinched-up eyes and tightly stretched lips would be interpreted as a friendly smile. But that proved to be the case. It was, after all, an obvious deduction. People in pain would not be bouncing around in public. They would be at home in bed, groaning, or at the doctor's office. It followed that my twisted expression was generally taken as a sign of cordiality. People responded to it.

"Who was that?" Herm would ask, as some complete stranger smiled and nodded to me in the street.

"I have no idea," I would say.

I glowed with new self-confidence, like a celebrity who is recognized and greeted wherever he goes. It would not have surprised me to be asked for my autograph. Our daily walks became triumphal processions.

"Wouldn't it be great," I said, "if we could all smile at one another and the whole world be happy?"

"Within reason, within reason," Herm said. He is inclined to be cautious.

Of course he is right. I can think of a number of people whose smiles I would not return.

As the days passed, I came to believe that everyone in town was my friend. My soul expanded. Herm commented on my new benevolence.

"You are mellowing, my dear," he said.

I did not care for his choice of words, but let it pass.

It was all very well to stumble along the street hanging on to Herm and receiving greetings from people who probably thought they must have met me somewhere but couldn't quite remember. But I had to do more than this. I had to get into my car.

For me, driving is as essential as breathing. Herm says that is a ridiculous statement so I will modify it by saying "almost as essential." I love my car the way a glutton loves food. In fact, I would rather drive than eat. It would take a lot more than uncomfortable contact lenses to keep me for long from my favorite perch behind the wheel. I decided to drive down to the breakwater and paint sailboats.

Every beginning artist in this town spends hours at the harbor painting sailboats and fishing boats and palm trees in the distance. The market is glutted with paintings of our harbor. I figured one more by me would not make much difference and it would be good practice. The art class I attend is full of harbor painters. It seems only polite to conform.

"Harbor, anyone?" I called to Herm, who was in the patio studying a seed catalog.

"I'd better come along," he said, "just to make sure you get there."

Driving without glasses on my nose gave me a feeling of confidence and power; I was now Superwoman. Nevertheless I drove with exaggerated caution, knowing that Herm was on the alert for danger.

"Don't go so fast!" he commanded as we proceeded at a less than hair-raising twenty-five miles per hour.

"Okay, Sweetie," I said cheerfully, as I continued at exactly the same speed. Superwoman was unflappable.

Herm was shocked into silence for a moment. Then he laughed.

"You've figured out how to deal with me, haven't you, Sugar?"

That's the way relationships change and develop. Unexpectedly, from trifles.

We reached the harbor without further incident. Herm helped me carry my easel and paintbox to a protected corner near the benches where, every day, a group of pretenders congregates.

"I'll just walk out to the end of the breakwater and see if there are any birds," Herm said, and off he went.

In other county seats the equivalent of this pretenders group would be found outside the courthouse, which is likely to be on a town square with benches and plenty of action to be observed and commented on. Our courthouse does not have these facilities, so the pretenders go to the harbor instead. They sit there for hours in their shabby old-fashioned clothes, sporting nautical caps that hint at a romantic seafaring past, for the benefit of strolling tourists, or else cowboy hats and braided thongs around their necks, pretend ranchers. All of this is only wistful dreaming and in real life they were salesmen in the hardware store or bookkeepers in a small dull office, but what harm is there in imagining?

They discuss the weather, past and present, their health, the city government, and the daily catch, which they watch being hauled in from the fishing boats. As the tourists, sailboat people, honeymooners, and kids with fishing poles go past, they observe them all. They turn their stiff necks to watch the pretty girls, in revealing undress, swing along, their dirty bare feet slapping down smartly.

The harbormaster sits in his office upstairs in the building behind the benches. He looks out at the activity around him and at intervals descends royally to go on a patrol boat around the harbor. As he emerges from his door, the bench sitters greet him as an old friend. It makes them feel important to be on a first-name basis with the harbormaster.

"Morning, Matt," they will say.

And he returns their greetings, genially, as he heads for his boat.

I set up my easel, aware of the pretenders muttering and coughing, rattling newspapers, smoking pipes full of cheap tobacco. It occurred to me that it would be more interesting to paint them than to do the sailboats that had really been done to death. I would call it *Old Men at the Harbor*. But not today. I had to learn to paint sailboats first.

The sun was making my eyes hurt more than usual and I was squinting fiercely, concentrating on trying not to weep, when my brush slipped out of my hand and rolled over next to the elastic-sided shoe of the pretend cowboy on the end of the nearest bench. He leaned over creakily to retrieve it, just as I stooped for it, and in so doing, knocked his hat off. I picked it up and handed it to him. He quickly clapped it back on his shiny pink head.

"Oh, I'm so sorry," I said.

"That's okay, missus. Here's your brush."

"Thank you."

Surely a harmless conversation, but he must have thought, from the involuntary leer on my face, that I was interested in striking up an acquaintance. He hauled himself to his feet, pulled his padded sleeveless jacket straight, and came over to look at my canvas. There wasn't much on it yet, just a few tentative squiggles. I tend to be timid at first, and advance gradually to bolder strokes.

"Nice day for painting sailboats," he offered.

"Yes. It surely is."

"Lots of painters come here."

"I'm sure they do."

"Some of them those hippie types, you know?"

"There are all kinds of painters," I said primly.

"I didn't mean for to be interruptin' you," he said. "Mind if I just watch for a minute? You go ahead and paint."

How could I tell him that I was unable to paint at all while he was looking over my shoulder? I made a few more squiggles but they were all wrong. The cowboy's pals on the bench kept glancing sideways at us and making comments that caused quiet laughter. Anyone, absolutely anyone, should have enough poise to deal with such a situation but not I, especially when I could scarcely see. I was reluctant to offend the cowboy, but I didn't know what to do or what to say to get rid of him. He stood there expectantly. I held my brush as though about to make a stroke of great significance. He was waiting to see it happen. It was an impasse.

I laid down the brush and rummaged in my pocket for a tissue to wipe my eyes.

Some passing tourists, seeing the cowboy watching me, stopped to look. One of them, a fat woman in green pajamas, looked at my canvas and patted my shoulder.

"Don't cry, dearie," she said. "Not everyone can be an artist."

"That's not why I'm crying," I told her. "It's these new contact lenses. I'm trying to get used to them."

"Oh," she said. "You want to be careful with those things. My sister-in-law got abrasions of the cornea from leaving them in too long. Very painful, it was."

She moved away.

"Some folks mighty free with advice," said the cowboy.

"She meant well," I said, looking up at him with my uncontrollable smile.

I tried again to make my brush do something dramatic and sensed that in addition to the cowboy on my left, I had another watcher on my right. It was Herm, who had come back from his walk. He had a proprietary air that was manifest to the cowboy, who backed off slightly.

"Howdy," he said to Herm.

"Howdy," Herm replied.

The cowboy tipped his hat to me.

"Nice talkin' to you, missus," he said, and returned to the bench.

"Ready to go?" Herm asked. He looked cross.

We packed up and went home. Herm knew perfectly well that my coquettish simper was not flirtatiousness but only a sign that my eyes hurt. Nevertheless, his instinctive reaction was quick and simple jealousy. My reaction, as atavistic as his, and fortunately as short-lived, was a female satisfaction at having made him jealous. Even people who know better can be very silly at times.

I went back, the next day, to Dr. Powell, who looks exactly like the Mock Turtle. He wrung his hands and said it was no use, my eyes were not adjusting properly.

"Maybe you should try soft lenses," he said. "They're less irritating for most people."

I thought of asking why he hadn't suggested that in the first place, but I knew the answer. He is simply a mossback who is slow to accept new ideas and doesn't really like the idea of contact lenses anyway.

"If you want to be fashionable, why don't you just get nice new frames?" he said.

He does not understand the difference between fashion and glamour. Many new fashions are just ludicrous and make women look ugly. But Herm sided with him.

"It's uncomfortable," he said, "living with a woman who is weeping all the time and making faces. I thought you looked fine before you ever got into this."

I was crushed, but only briefly. Having tasted freedom from the tyranny of glasses, I could never go back. Not without a struggle, anyway. I had read about soft lenses that had the advantage of requiring no breaking in and further-more, were actually disposable. At the end of a week or two they could be thrown away, which made unnecessary the nasty time-consuming job of cleaning them. Dr. Powell told me he did not carry them and would not prescribe them, be-cause they were something new. I am not sure whether such caution is lily-livered or just reactionary.

A little investigation in the Yellow Pages un-covered the Ribera Optometric Center, just down the hill from our house. It was presided over by a curly-headed young man (his picture was in the ad) named Dr. Zack O'Brien, and featured disposable soft lenses.

Dr. O'Brien's place proved to be a modest hole-in-the-wall squeezed between a dry cleaner and a take-out pizza shop. It would not have inspired confidence in the kind of people who felt secure in Dr. Powell's conservative office suite near the hospital. But I remembered the words of my good friend Sophocles: "One must learn by doing the thing: . . . you have no certainty, until you try." This was the advice I followed when I had my ears pierced, which was an irreversible act. Getting disposable lenses would not be irreversible. I could return to the old glasses at any time.

The new lenses are so marvelously comfortable that I am not even aware of their presence. Because I no longer make faces, people in the street don't smile at me any more. Herm is happy about that. He never really believed that the pretend ranchers and sea captains were a threat, but there are other mature gentlemen, in snappy sport jackets, strolling about. And as I have told him, one should never take a woman for granted.

15

Mr. McVitty
and the Dustbins

One thing we have in abundance here in Los Barcos is civic pride. We support with enthusiasm a disproportionate number of paint stores and plant nurseries. Even the mailboxes on the main street downtown are hidden in containers adorned with Mexican tiles and surrounded by beds of jasmine. When we talk about Beautiful Los Barcos, we expect to be taken seriously.

There was, therefore, some concern when a house just two doors from us was sold to a man who proposed to use it as a rental property. Rental properties are looked upon with disfavor by neighboring homeowners, for obvious reasons. There was even more concern when, after a slapdash paint job, which changed the original white to a sickly yellow, the first tenants moved in.

They arrived in a pickup truck and a van, loaded with mattresses, dogs, and macramé plant hangers. They were soon joined by friends in decrepit cars that crowded the driveway and spilled into the street. The house began to take on the woebegone aspect of a camp for undesirables.

Just as Herm and I were preparing to launch a campaign against the free-roving dogs, they and their owners disappeared and a new cast took over. Gradually we became aware of a continual coming and going at the yellow house, of a company in perpetual motion, like the waves of the sea advancing and receding, never still.

The residents of the street became accustomed to it. There was no use objecting to the laundry draped over the balcony rail, or the unmowed grass, because chances were that in a week or two the laundry would be replaced by hanging plants and the grass would have a tent pitched on it. Before the authorities could be called in to deal with the tent, it would have been dismantled and its occupants gone. Our only hope was that the owner of the place was finding it difficult to collect the rent and would eventually sell the house to someone who would live in it and keep it tidy. Meanwhile we tried to ignore it.

In Los Barcos the garbage is collected twice a week very early in the morning, and the collection fee is based on whether the customer wants the collector to go around to the back of his house where the trash cans are hidden, or whether he is willing to trundle them out to the curb himself. In the latter case, there is an ordinance stating that the cans cannot be placed at the curb until eight o'clock the night before the collection, and must be taken in by ten in the morning of collection day.

On our street everyone except the tenants of the yellow house paid to have the garbage collector go around to the back of the house. The yellow house people had two dented sagging galvanized cans which stood out in front, beside the driveway, day after day, and were frequently overturned by nocturnal animals. The McVittys, living next door to us, and thereby immediately adjacent to the yellow house, were understandably distressed.

"It's an outrage, that's what it is," Mr. McVitty told Herm one day.

They were both out in their respective gardens, and I heard the conversation through an open window. Mr. McVitty is an Englishman who retired to Los Barcos and has spent the last ten years coaxing his garden into perfection. He is a charming, gentle person with pink cheeks and wispy white hair.

"I thought perhaps they didn't know the rules

here," he said to Herm. "A lot of them have license plates from other states. So I decided to go over and explain."

"That took courage," Herm said.

"I went over at five o'clock yesterday afternoon," Mr. McVitty said. "This young chap and a girl, both with bare feet, came to the door, and I started to explain about the dustbins, but they said . . . they said . . ."

He was so indignant that he could barely speak.

"The fellow said, 'Don't bother us. We're busy doing our thing.' "

"I said, 'What do you mean, doing your thing?' He said, 'We're artists.' And he closed the door. What cheek!"

"What we should do is get the city to send an inspector over to issue a warning," Herm said. "After all, it *is* in violation of a city ordinance."

"That's a splendid idea," Mr. McVitty said. "I wonder, Mr. Herman, if you would undertake to make the call. With my accent, they might think it's some foreigner trying to cause trouble."

It took Herm two days to reach the right person in the Department of Public Works. Either the line was busy or there was no answer. We suspect they leave the telephone off the hook much of the time and replace it when they go for their coffee breaks. The inspector, when cornered, promised to come over as soon as possible but could not say when that would be. Perhaps in a few days.

However, on Saturday morning I happened to be driving past the yellow house and I saw the artist couple, assisted by a group of friends, loading a mattress, a heap of clothing, and some canvases into a rusted van. They were moving out.

That afternoon another van arrived. It disgorged three young men, a couple of mattresses, and a potter's wheel. By Sunday the dustbins had been filled with clay and removed from the curb to the garage where the young men were busily making pottery. The garage door, as always, was wide open, and the potters were completely nude.

Mrs. McVitty telephoned.

"Oh Lydia," she said in her clear chirping voice, "what shall we do? It's a scandal."

"Well, I'm not sure," I said. "We didn't have much luck with the garbage can—I mean—dustbin inspector, and we'll have to find out who the nudity inspector is."

"It would be the police," Herm said when I told him about it.

But Herm and I were reluctant to call the police. There had been a recent epidemic of burglaries and purse snatchings and we did not want to distract even one policeman from the important task of apprehending criminals. The burglars, we felt, were dangerous; the nudists, just silly. Besides, they would probably move away soon, like the other tenants of the yellow house.

In the garden, Mr. McVitty commented on the situation to Herm.

"Well, the dustbins are gone, but as I said to my wife, 'What you win on the swings is lost upon the roundabouts.' "

"Er, yes," Herm said.

It took five weeks for the potters to decide that Los Barcos was not a fertile field for their enterprise. The truth was, we already had too many potters and not enough customers to support them all. They piled their equipment and unsold pots into the van and drove away. A sigh of relief, like a fresh breeze, floated up and down the street.

The yellow house was vacant for two weeks, during which time the Los Barcos Janitorial Service truck was seen there for a couple of days. Then an old station wagon, dragging a rental move-yourself trailer, turned up. It was unloaded by a man of about thirty with long hair on his face and none on his head, which made him look as though his hair had just slid down. He was accompanied by an untidy woman and a pretty two-year-old child. They had brought an assortment of shabby furniture and several large stained glass panels, which they immediately hung in the windows.

The next day, the battered garbage cans were out in front again, and there they remained.

Herm and I held a back fence conference with the McVittys. We agreed that no help would be forthcoming from the Gudges across from us. Only their back garden faced our street and they were therefore not really affected. The house next door to us on the other side belonged to the rock music-barbecue people, from whom no co-operation could be expected. Across from them was the lady who spoke no English.

"What they do in the Midwest," I said, "is, when new people move in, the neighbors go to call on them and take little gifts, like a home-made pie, or something."

"They don't do things like that in California," Mrs. McVitty said sadly.

"No they don't, but that's all the more reason why it would be a good idea," I said.

"I could make some of those cookies that Mr. Herman liked so much when he broke his leg," Mrs. McVitty said.

"That would be lovely," I said. "And we could take over a bunch of Herm's roses."

We decided to go together and two days later,

at eleven in the morning, Mrs. McVitty and I walked up to the yellow house. The door was opened by the young woman, who was wearing jeans and a T-shirt but had not yet combed her hair. The child was sitting on the floor putting clothespins into a cornflakes box and then dumping them out again..

"Hello," I said. "I'm Lydia Herman and this is Mrs. McVitty. We're from just down the street, and we want to welcome you to Plaza de los Rosales."

I held out the bunch of roses—they were really gorgeous ones, Sutter's Gold with a heavenly fragrance—and Mrs. McVitty proffered a foil plate of cookies, neatly covered with plastic wrap.

"Susie Miller," said the woman, accepting the gifts, "and this is Deodar Cedar. Dee Dee for short. We named her that because of where she was conceived."

Mrs. McVitty turned red and then squeaked, "In a tree?"

"No, no. *Under* the tree," Susie Miller said. "Come on in and sit down."

We advanced a few steps and I saw that the only chairs were of the beanbag variety. I knew that if Mrs. McVitty should sit in one, we would have to lift her out, rather embarrassing for such a dignified old lady.

"Thank you, no. We can't stay," I said, as we backed to the door. "But I just did want to tell you about an ordinance here that you probably haven't heard about yet."

"In regard to the dustbins," Mrs. McVitty said, smiling sweetly.

Susie Miller looked puzzled.

"The garbage cans," I said. "They are supposed to be taken in by ten A.M. on collection day, and not put out until eight in the evening before the next collection."

"Oh, really?"

"Perhaps when your husband comes home you could explain it to him," I said.

"Oh, Gary's not my husband," Susie said. "I'll tell him what you said, but he's not likely to do anything about it and he would be angry if I did."

We goggled in astonishment.

"He's out looking for a job now," Susie said, "because my folks have threatened to stop sending checks. But he probably won't find one because he deliberately antagonizes people."

"Now why would he do that?" Mrs. McVitty said.

"I don't know," Susie said. "It has something to do with following the laws of God rather than the laws of man but I don't entirely understand it."

"Dear, oh dear," said Mrs. McVitty.

"You see, if the street inspector comes, you'll be fined," I said.

"Well, thank you very much for the presents, and the advice," Susie said, "It was nice meeting you. Say bye-bye, Dee Dee."

"Bye-bye," Dee Dee said.

We left.

"She seemed a pleasant enough young woman," I said to Mrs. McVitty as we walked home, "but I guess Dee Dee's father is some sort of nut."

"This Gary may not even *be* Dee Dee's father," Mrs. McVitty said. "Imagine naming a child Deodar Cedar! Dear, oh dear."

That afternoon we held another over-the-fence conference with the McVittys.

Herm suggested that Gary might be easier to deal with if he had a job.

"Being unemployed often makes people antisocial," he said.

We stood in the sunshine and pondered this.

"There's a meeting of the Los Barcos Lunch Club tomorrow," Herm said. "I think I'll ask Ralph Lotz if he knows of any jobs."

Ralph Lotz is a local contractor and currently chairman of the Beautiful Los Barcos Committee. Herm goes to these lunch meetings because they have interesting speakers and it gives him a chance to talk with people he has known for years but would not otherwise see. Sort of like me with the Happy Girls and their monthly coffees.

Since we had no idea what skills, if any, Gary possessed, Herm could not recommend him to Mr. Lotz in any specific way, but said that judging by the stained glass in the windows and the name of the child, he was clearly an artistic person.

"Lotz seemed pleased," Herm reported that evening. "He said they've been trying to get a young person onto the committee, someone who could establish rapport with the residents of the campus area, but the pay isn't much."

"I think even a little pay would be welcome at the yellow house," I said.

A couple of days later, when I went out to the mailbox, I saw Susie in the street taking a walk with Dee Dee.

"Gary has a part-time job now," she told me. "He's on the Beautiful Los Barcos Committee. It will help until he finds something permanent."

"That's great," I said.

"He thought about it for a couple of hours before he accepted it," Susie said. "But finally he decided that it was not against the laws of God to beautify the city."

"A wise decision," I said.

Later that day, when we drove past the yellow house, we saw that the garbage cans were no longer in evidence.

For a couple of weeks all was serene, and then one afternoon I overheard Mr. McVitty call to Herm out in the garden.

"I say, Mr. Herman, you'll want to hear this. Yesterday I put a load of garden trash in the dustbin and left it near the curb to be picked up this morning, because it was all from that front part of the garden and I saw no point in hauling it to the back of my house, and that fellow Gary came rushing over and told me that I couldn't put the dustbin out until eight in the evening."

"No kidding?" Herm said.

"Mind you, he was polite about it," Mr. McVitty said, "but firm. He showed me his Beautiful Los Barcos badge. I was a bit annoyed, you know, but he offered to move it for me, and of course he was in the right."

"There is none so zealous as the recent convert," Herm said.

He began to laugh and after a moment Mr. McVitty laughed, too.

16

Many Fine Bargains

The Gudges' house across the street is on a lot that goes clear through from Rosebush Plaza to Via La Loma, which winds down the hill into town. The bougainvillea-covered fence enclosing their back garden is mostly obscured by the assortment of broken-down cars and trucks that Mr. Gudge lines up along the curb, forcing our friends to park far down the block. He used to work on only one at a time but now he has at least six and no sooner does he sell one than he replaces it with another, so that we are always confronted by a collection of rusty derelicts.

Herm says I mean "affronted," not "confronted." He feels strongly that Mr. Gudge's business, or hobby, should not be conducted in the street, where it gives offense to the neighbors. But we have hesitated to report him for parking violations because, although we have never enjoyed even the slightest rapport with the Gudges, we prefer to avoid open conflict. I agree with Herm that the disemboweled vehicles are no asset to the neighborhood, but personally feel much more outraged by the alternate-lifestyle people in the next block, whose underfed dogs are, despite the leash law, permitted to roam at large and sometimes threaten to attack when I go down to the mailbox. At least Mr. Gudge's cars just sit there, peacefully.

When Mr. Gudge is not tinkering with his cars, he is working in his garden. He has a tiny orchard behind his house and an everchanging variety of flowers in front, on the Via La Loma side.

Of course it is all a matter of taste, but Mr. Gudge's ideas on landscaping seem to us a bit bizarre. In the center of his front lawn is a conventional birdbath with a naked lady rising gracefully from the bowl and holding aloft a spray of artificial flowers, which Mr. Gudge changes from time to time as it gradually becomes bedraggled. One day, when driving home up the hill, we were astonished to see that the birdbath had been further enhanced by a collection of rocks arranged around it on the lawn, all painted, patriotically, red, white, and blue.

"I think I'd rather look at the old cars than at

those rocks," I remarked to Herm. "Still, it shows that he cares."

Herm views Mr. Gudge with distrust because several times when I have gone to the mailbox Mr. Gudge has detached himself from the innards of the vehicle under repair and has come over to me offering gallant compliments on how well I am looking and sometimes springing to open the mailbox door for me. All he needs is a plumed hat.

He cooled off for a while after the affair of the cow but eventually he forgave us. I can't always understand everything he says because he mumbles, but the leers are unmistakable.

"How can you possibly like him?" Herm said. "He has dirty teeth."

That's a terrible thing to say about anyone. I decided it would be best to ask Herm to fetch the mail whenever Mr. Gudge was out in the street.

One day, on our way home from the supermarket, we saw that a large handlettered sign had been planted in Mr. Gudge's front lawn. It read "MANY FINE BARGAINS."

"What do you suppose he is selling?" I said.

"Junk," said Herm.

"It would be fun to go and see," I persisted. "I've always wondered what the inside of that house is like."

"Junk," Herm repeated.

"We wouldn't have to buy anything."

"You go ahead, if you want to, but leave me out of it," Herm said.

He sounded so cross that I dropped the subject, but I kept wondering.

On the second day after the planting of the sign, Herm had gone downtown and I was at home when the mailman came. I hurried out to the box, expecting, as always, something wonderful—a letter from the children, perhaps, or a notice that I had won a million dollars, or a free sample of bubble bath.

Mr. Gudge looked up as I approached.

"Hello, missus," he said, smiling broadly.

"Hello, Mr. Gudge," I said. "Nice day."

I opened the mailbox and pulled out a handful of bills, advertising circulars, and an alumni magazine from the college Herm's son Mike had attended briefly fifteen years ago.

Mr. Gudge had sidled closer as I inspected the mail. When I looked up, there he was, just three feet away.

"You want some bargains?" he said.

If there had been just one thing of interest in that mailbox, even a bird-walk announcement from the Audubon Society, I would have said no thank you and gone back up the driveway. But the bundle of unwanted paper in my hand made me feel depressed, and when I feel depressed I behave stupidly.

"What kind of bargains?" I said.

Mr. Gudge waved his arms grandly.

"All kinds," he said. "Furniture, dishes, paintings, you come and look."

I can't help it. Houses fascinate me. I realized that this was probably the only opportunity I would ever have to see the Gudges' house.

"Well, I'm awfully busy right now," I said, "but I guess I could spare a minute."

Mr. Gudge is a tall, skinny man, slightly stooped. He opened the high gate and ushered me into his orchard. We walked around the house to the front door and entered a small, dark hall, to the left of which was a small, dark living room heaped with the so-called bargains. A folding picnic table had been set up in front of the fireplace and on it was an assortment of rubbish. Mr. Gudge waved me toward the table.

The only thing of interest in the jumble of cloudy jelly glasses and cracked dishes was a set of crocheted antimacassars. Those, I thought, might have some value as antiques, in another fifty years. There were price tags on everything, including most of the furniture in the room.

Mr. Gudge pointed proudly to a sofa and chair that combined brutally carved wood with brown plush upholstery. It was not the Victoriana that today is so highly prized. It was just old and ugly.

"Now that my wife has the decorating shop," he said, "she wants to change everything here. I tell her new stuff is not so good but she won't listen."

I stood near the picnic table, wondering what to do next.

"I know that *you*, missus, would appreciate these fine-quality pieces. Sit in the chair. Try it," Mr. Gudge said.

I sat on the edge of the chair, just to please him. It was rock-hard and the plush was scratchy.

"It's very nice, but I'm afraid it wouldn't look right in my house," I said.

Mr. Gudge looked sad.

"I thought if you bought it, the chair and sofa, it wouldn't be so far away. Maybe you would let me come to look at it sometimes."

"You must be greatly attached to these things, Mr. Gudge. Were they in your family?"

"My mother," said Mr. Gudge.

He indicated a framed photograph on the wall. I jumped up and went to look at it. It showed a young woman dressed in dark silk with lots of tiny buttons. What I coveted was the oval frame, but it was not for sale.

"She was very beautiful," I said, although she wasn't, especially.

"Yes."

He looked so downcast that I thought I would have to buy something to cheer him up. I returned to the table with the idea of finding the cheapest object and then leaving. I picked up a badly designed pitcher, small with a large square lip. It was tagged at fifty cents. I figured I could consider the fifty cents as an admission fee to view the house. On the other hand, I had seen nothing but the hall and the living room. You've been had, Lydia, I said to myself. I would have to promise to pay later, as I had no money with me, and that would entail another encounter with Mr. Gudge, something which I hoped to avoid.

The jangle of the doorbell saved me. Mr. Gudge turned away and went to the door, where two of those frowsy women who haunt garage sales stood smiling with shopping bags.

There actually are women who spend all their time going from garage sale to moving sale to yard sale to swap meet, coming away with pottery salt shakers in animal shapes, cracked mirrors, faded plastic jewelry, the jetsam of other lives. It is a harmless modus vivendi and there is something to be said for it. It gets them out into the fresh air and may lead to interesting social situations.

They pushed past Mr. Gudge and as they did

so, I said "Good-bye, Mr. Gudge. I must go now," and hurried out.

Herm had arrived home while I was gone.

"Where were you?" he asked as I came in. "I didn't see you when I drove up."

"Just getting the mail," I said, waving the crumpled papers at him. "And then I stopped in to see the bargains across the street."

"Did you buy something?"

"No," I said. "You were right. It was all just junk. And the house is not a bit nice inside."

A few days later I was doing an errand on Ribera Street when Mrs. Gudge came to the door of her shop, Gloria's Grotto for Gracious Interiors.

"Good morning, Mrs. Herman," she called.

I stopped and returned her greeting.

"My husband said you came over to our sale."

"Yes," I said. "But the only thing I could use was not for sale. That framed picture of Mr. Gudge's mother."

"Mr. Gudge's mother?"

"Yes. I liked the frame. But of course I didn't realize it was a family treasure."

Mrs. Gudge looked at me sharply.

"We have no picture of Mr. Gudge's mother," she said. "The one you're talking about is something I picked up in a secondhand shop last year. *I* liked the frame, too."

"Well," I said, embarrassed, "I guess Mr. Gudge was just joking when he told me that, ha ha."

I started to sidle away.

"I'll try to find you one like it," Mrs. Gudge said, "now that I'm in the business."

But I had had enough of the Gudges.

"Thank you, no," I said. "I really don't have any place to put it."

It was cocktail time when I got home. We took our drinks out to the balcony and sat there reading the evening paper and enjoying the view. I told Herm about the picture of Mr. Gudge's mother.

He chortled with satisfaction.

"I told you the fellow was a rascal, didn't I, Sugar?" he said, and looked as pleased as though he had won a prize at the rose show.

17

The Health
of Fred Tucker

When Herm and I moved to this neighborhood we began to patronize the service
station at the foot of the hill. The proprietor,
Fred Tucker, was a fiftyish bachelor who quickly
learned to know us and the peculiarities of our
two cars.

Fred was a tall man with thinning dark hair, a
red face, and an unusually large nose. He had
squinty eyes under bushy black eyebrows. His
hands were always black with auto grease, some
of which occasionally smeared on his cheek. If
people were judged solely by appearance, Fred
would have a low rating except when he smiled.

Whether Fred really loved all his customers is
open to question, but when he smiled at them,
which he usually did, they responded like flowers
in the morning sunlight. I knew one woman who
used him as a therapist. Whenever she had a

fight with her husband she would go to Fred's, where she indulged in tears and a can of soda pop while Fred, turning the gas pump over to one of the boys, spoke soothing words and patted her shoulder, leaving black smudges.

On weekends Fred left the station in the care of his two employees, high school boys, and went hiking in remote places. During the week, he devoted his evenings to dates with various ladies of his acquaintance.

Fred took his girlfriends to lectures, about which he was always cheerfully voluble.

"Well, did you have a big time last night, Fred?" I always asked him when I stopped for gas.

"Oh, it was very nice," Fred would answer. "We went to a most interesting lecture about the digestive system. Did you know that only two or three—"

I never found out what he was going to say on that occasion because just then one of the boys dropped the hose and gasoline began to spill out on the ground. Fred sprang to the rescue and by the time it was mopped up I was on my way out.

He reported on lectures entitled "Live with Your Lungs," "Be Kind to Your Kidneys," and "New Vistas in Heart Disease." I felt sorry for the women who were so lonely and desperate for an evening out that they accepted these programs as dates, and hoped that after the lecture they would perhaps do something more entertaining, if not entirely put off by gloomy reflections.

I suppose Fred benefited from those lectures, because he certainly looked healthy, but Herm said it was probably the hiking.

After a while I noticed that when Fred spoke of his dates he was referring to "my friend" instead of "one of the ladies I know."

"I think he's narrowed it down to one woman," I told Herm. "Maybe he's thinking of getting married."

"Bachelors that age never get married," Herm said. "Why should they? They don't know what they're missing and they like to boast about their freedom."

But one morning when I stopped for gas, the pump was attended by a stocky middle-aged woman in a blue shirt and jeans. On the shirt pocket was her name, Arlene. Some potted geraniums that had never been there before were placed around the edges of the station and a red-and-white striped awning had been installed over the office door.

Fred saw me and came out.

"Morning, Mrs. Herman. I want you to meet my new partner, Arlene. We tied the knot last

Saturday, up on the Laurel Mountain trail. Had our friends there and Reverend Nelson from Arlene's church."

I got out of the car to shake hands and offer congratulations as they stood beaming at each other. Arlene's smile was just as warm as Fred's.

"Arlene wants to help out at the station," Fred said as he cleaned the windshield. "Now I won't be so dependent on those pesky boys."

One morning when I stopped for gas I said, "Well, Fred, I haven't heard about any health lectures recently. I suppose now that you're married, you prefer to stay home in the evenings."

"Well, it's this way, Mrs. Herman," he said, polishing the little side mirror so vigorously that I could tell he was pushing it out of alignment. "Arlene is a great music lover and she's teaching me to play the recorder. We play duets, you know. It's very nice."

"There's lots of good music you can play on the recorder," I said.

"That's what Arlene says. She thinks I have talent. And she said she was getting tired of the lectures anyway."

"Well, Fred, Shakespeare said, 'If music be the food of love, play on.' "

About a month after Fred's wedding, Herm and I stopped for gas, and as we drove away Herm said, "That's what I was afraid of. A man that age gets married, next thing you know he has a heart attack."

"He didn't look well, did he?" I said. "Overdoing, I suppose."

"In more ways than one, very likely," Herm said. "Fellow ought to have more sense."

At that moment a surfer in a jeep painted with psychedelic designs shot out of a side street right in front of us. Herm reached over and leaned on the horn, producing an earsplitting noise that frightened me more than the surfer. Before I got the new contact lenses I would have been angry and perhaps snapped at him, but now I merely said, "Thank you, darling" as though I would have done it myself if he hadn't.

Fred's genial personality continued as usual to charm his customers, but his red face became paler and finally almost blue.

"How's the music?" I asked him one day.

He shook his head.

"I don't think I have as much talent as Arlene says. And I feel so tired in the evenings."

"Better take care of yourself, Fred. Maybe you should start going to those health lectures again."

His face brightened.

"Matter of fact, we're going to one tonight. It's called 'Don't Belittle Your Blood Pressure.' "

"That's a good title," I said. "Hope you enjoy it."

With just the normal amount of driving around town one tankful of gas lasts quite a while in my little car, so it was a whole week before I saw Fred again. His complexion seemed to have regained a bit of its former ruddiness, and he had bounce in his step. He greeted me with more than usual ebullience.

"Say, Mrs. Herman, you should have heard the lecture we went to last night. All about glaucoma."

He scraped some bug juice off the windshield.

"You know, I really enjoyed it!"

"Did Arlene like it too?"

"Oh yes," he said. "That's why we get along so well. We both enjoy the same things."

I could see Arlene standing in the office doorway watching. From the expression on her face I knew Fred was going to be all right.

18

Faith Without Works

The dog population of this city can be divided into two categories: (1) Dogs that love me and (2) Others.

My relationship with Bonnie, the basset hound next door, is one of mutual affection and trust. Bonnie is officially confined to a fenced-in backyard, but she has dug a hole under her fence and through our hedge and often comes to visit when I am out in the garden. Whenever I see her waddling in my direction I am reminded of Mrs. Honeycott, a woman of remarkable embonpoint who presides over our local choral society with imperious manner and a heart of mush. Bonnie has much the same build and disposition. She slobbers kisses on me while I pat her head and tell her how much I love her. She is even more enthusiastic about Herm, which makes me just a teensy bit jealous.

Some of my friends have dogs who are also friends of mine. Each one has identified me as a softy and, ignoring everyone else, comes begging, lays his head on my knee, and turns on a piteous can't-you-see-I'm-starving expression when the potato chips are passed. This cuts down on the number of calories I consume, so it's a good thing all round.

No, I have no trouble with the dogs that know me. But they number only five in this whole city. It is the Others that create the problem.

The truth is that I am terrified of dogs that bark and dash about flaunting their fangs. The dogs, of course, know it. They have devised a secret system of communication so that every day when Herm and I go for our walk, the dogs are informed in advance that we are on the way, and just what territory we shall cover. As a result, normally quiet streets and empty parks suddenly harbor fierce animals. Often they pretend to be asleep as other people pass them. But they are only lying in ambush. As Herm and I approach, they spring up and rush at me, slavering, like Spenser's "hungry Spaniells with greedy jawes, Her ready for to teare." Time after time I have had an astounded and embarrassed dog owner assure me that his dog has *never* done that before, and I believe him.

"Pay no attention," says Herm, holding my

hand tightly both to give me reassurance and to keep me from making matters worse by running.

"Down, boy!" he says severely.

He raises his arm as if to throw a rock, and the animal, having had his fun, retreats. Although my legs have turned to jelly and my heart is pounding, I stagger along, supported by Herm, and gradually return to normal.

I am not paranoid. I just know for a fact that the dogs of this city are united in a conspiracy against me.

So it was with much interest that I read in a Helpful Hints column the following: To repel vicious dogs, use a solution of one part ammonia to three parts water in a water pistol and squirt the dog between the eyes. This will not cause permanent damage to the dog but will instantly stop him.

The local toy store supplied me with a little black plastic water pistol, but Herm was uneasy about it.

"It's dangerous," he said, "to go about in public carrying anything that looks like a gun. You might get in trouble with the police. You might get into a fracas with someone with a real gun. Or something."

Back at the toy store, I bought a larger water pistol of bright orange plastic. It looked anything *but* real, and Herm thought it would be permissible. I filled it with the ammonia-water mix and practiced in the patio, aiming between the eyes of a stone frog who lives under the mimosa tree.

"Now we're in business," I chortled, swaggering up and down with a Matt Dillon swivel that worried Herm a little.

"Lydia my darling, please don't wiggle like that in the street."

Out in the street, however, I was not quite so confident. In addition, I felt rather foolish walking about with the orange gun, which could not be put in a pocket because it was too big and besides, it leaked.

We had gone only two blocks on our first armed excursion when a mongrel, menacing, blocked our way. It was the moment of truth. I raised the gun, pulled the trigger, and stood in delighted astonishment as the animal turned and ran.

By the next day, the word had been passed along. Canine radar, I suppose. Leave her alone, she's armed to the teeth. The sudden lack of interest in me, on the part of the dogs, was almost insultingly ostentatious.

It was lovely. Herm and I felt free to walk anywhere, so long as I had a firm grip on my pistol. I always filled it before leaving the house and tested it on the stone frog. The dogs remained in hiding and I had no further occasion to use it, but my faith in its power continued unabated.

One day Herm and I were walking on the beach. Signs sprout all over the sand saying No Dogs Allowed on Beach, but there are usually twenty dogs for every sign. However, we wanted to welcome back the willets, whimbrels, and godwits that we hadn't seen all summer, so we decided to chance it.

It was a cloudy day and rather cool. Not many people on the beach. The shorebirds were there and we said hello to them. We were startled by the sound of barking.

Coming toward us were a leather-skinned witch and her familiar, a monster that resembled the hound of the Baskervilles. This animal had not received the message about my weaponry; perhaps he had been out of town. He ran toward me, no longer barking but worse, snarling. Coolly I raised the pistol, took aim, and fired. No liquid squirted, not a drop. I tried again. It was jammed. The witch stood by, sneering. Herm was furious.

"Call off your dog!" he shouted to her.

She growled something to the dog and they continued on their way.

"Well, back to square one," I said to Herm. "It was nice, having faith."

"Yes. But faith without works is dead. James, chapter two, verse twenty," Herm said, and dropped the orange gun into a trash barrel in the parking lot.

"Never mind, Sugar. I'll protect you," he said.

Dear Herm. Of course he will.

19

The Benefit

When the City Council decided to go ahead with the renovation of an old section downtown, their action threatened to displace a thrift shop called The Doghouse, whose proceeds were used to neuter the dogs and cats brought in by indigent citizens and operated on by local veterinarians who contributed their services.

The staff consisted entirely of volunteer workers, who were kept busy arranging, pricing, and selling the cast-off furniture and clothing that was donated.

Mrs. Paterson, a woman I know slightly, was working there the day I went in with an armload of blouses that I was bored with. She thanked me for the blouses and said, "I wish we could get more men's clothing. Doesn't your husband—?"

"Herm expects all his clothes to last forever

and he never gets tired of them," I told her. "In fact, the older a thing is, the better he likes it."

Mrs. Paterson sighed.

"I'm afraid a lot of men are like that," she said. "An old shirt or jacket is sort of a security blanket."

She twitched some ornaments on the counter.

"The real moneymaker is the knickknacks, stuff like this. You wouldn't believe the things people will buy." She shook her head. "Last week I sold a picture of four puppies dressed up in fancy clothes, sitting at a table playing bridge. For ten dollars!"

"Maybe the person bought it for the frame," I said.

"No. The frame was broken."

I made appropriate clucking sounds and a mental note to bring in a pair of candlesticks made of seashells that still smelled of the original occupants. They had been given to me by one of Herm's nephew's former girlfriends.

"Our problem now," Mrs. Paterson said, "is finding the money to move to another location. We never have any surplus funds, and you know how expensive moving is."

My friend Poppy, although a fanatical animal lover and supporter of The Doghouse, has always been such a dithery, confused person that I was astonished when she was named chairman of the committee to raise money. No doubt they couldn't find anyone else to do it and Poppy, now entirely taken up with her new boyfriend, Wilfred—she calls him Wilfie, which I think is disgusting—did not realize what she was in for. Egged on by other Doghouse supporters, she agreed to organize a benefit and stopped in to ask if I would design some posters to advertise it.

"Of course," I said. "Be glad to. What is the program?"

Poppy looked slightly embarrassed.

"We were thinking of having a poetry reading."

"You're putting me on," I said.

I enjoy these new slangy expressions, although Herm's granddaughter Sandra has told me gently that they are usually out of date by the time I catch up with them.

One of the committee members had a son who was "into" poetry (that's another one of those new expressions), and the son had a couple of like-minded friends. Most of them had guitars. The only difficulty was that some of the poets disapproved of the work done by The Doghouse, maintaining that it was better for an animal's mental health to allow it to reproduce freely. But when asked what would happen to all the unwanted offspring, they had no practical answers. Anyway, the lure of reading to a paying audience proved irresistible.

The committee rented the basement room of an impoverished church, and I got to work on the posters. One of the poets called himself Long Fellow, a conceit that I felt could be used to advantage. The older people would mistake it for the name of a poet popular in the classrooms of their youth. The young people would recognize Long Fellow as one of their own. In between would be quite a few who would interpret the name as a promise of X-rated entertainment and cheaper than the movies.

I designed the poster with the poet's name in large black letters, LONG FELLOW. If they noticed it at all, the old folks would construe the space between the G and the F as a mistake on the part of the printer. Herm said that was unethical but I didn't think so. Still, it is a fine point.

One bewildered lady, who had read the poster hastily, somehow got the idea that Long Fellow was the name of a performing dachshund, who would do his act between poems.

The benefit was scheduled for four o'clock on a Saturday afternoon. It was one of those cool overcast days we often get in early June. Herm and I arrived early in order to get seats near the front. We had never been to a poetry reading and did not want to miss anything.

The surroundings were uninspiring, even, one might say, grim. Walls, ceiling, and floor were painted battleship gray. Rows of folding wooden chairs labeled Courtesy of Glenn Whittle Plumbing had been set up facing the end wall, with space left for the performers. There was no stage. We sat in the third row and looked around.

Three young mothers in trash-can dresses sat across the aisle. They carried, around their necks, cloth bags into which babies were stuffed. I am told this is the correct way to do it now and that the babies love it. The mothers were discussing a new health food book, which one of them produced from her satchel. I could overhear frequent repetition of the one word in the English language that makes me feel queasy. The word is "yogurt." I swallowed hard and looked away.

A group of dignified people, whose conversation identified them as members of the Silver Fun Club, sat behind us.

Poppy, in a long red dress that helped relieve the gloom, bustled in with two of her committee members, all carrying wooden crates that they arranged in the performing area for the poets to stand or sit on.

The room was filling up with well-dressed citizens who acted as though they were doing their good deed for the day before going on to cocktail parties. Some of them, obviously, had already been to a party. Scattered about were small groups of young men who had achieved complete anonymity by disguising themselves as Old English sheepdogs. They were accompanied by tattered young women bearing up bravely despite evidences of dire poverty—bare feet and complete absence of underwear. Herm was impressed by their courage in remaining cheerful under the circumstances.

"It's not poverty, it's the fashion," I told him.

He didn't believe me and I wasn't surprised. If normally you are oblivious to fashion, you are bound to be jolted when occasionally you look around and see what is going on. Of course we always saw people like this at the college music recitals, but on the campus one expects it and pays no attention.

Poppy clapped her hands to command silence and announced that the first reading would be by Jonathan Gibbon, accompanied on the guitar by—she squinted at the paper—by David Mumble. (At least it sounded like Mumble.)

One of the sheepdogs, carrying papers, ambled to the front and stood on a crate. David Mumble sat on another crate nearby, with his guitar.

Mumble immediately proved that he knew

little or nothing about guitar playing but had come only to support his friend. He strummed with graceful hands and produced twangy noises, after which Jonathan Gibbon, pausing now and then for a twang from Mumble, read the following:

> I writhe.
> In leaf the sea, go, go.

Twang.

> Oh world of worms
> Rise, writhe,
> Worms that carriage softly harshly mainly
>   ungainly.

Twang.

> Ha!
> Will the mandrill speak?

He smiled and bowed to mild applause. Mumble stood and bowed, then resumed his seat on the crate.

Behind me a Silver Fun Club gentleman asked his wife, "What was that about?"

"I don't know, dear," she said. "It's modern poetry."

Gibbon rustled his papers and read another poem. It was much like the first one, punctuated by twangs from Mumble and having to do with dripping blood. I could not understand whose blood it was or why it was dripping, but it was distinctly unpleasant and caused a good deal of foot shuffling in the Silver Fun Club section and some giggles from the cocktail party set.

Herm was getting to look bored and irritated, which meant that soon he would whisper "Let's go" and we would have to walk out under the reproachful eyes of Poppy and the poets.

The next poet was the one called Long Fellow. He was short and fat, more like a teddy bear than a sheepdog. He put one foot on a crate, rested his guitar on his thigh, and produced twangs like Mumble's, only louder.

"What is love?" he shouted.

"Polluted like the air,

Filthy like the ocean."

Twang.

"With nuclear wastes loathsome."

Twang. And louder, TWANG TWANG.

"Comical!" he bellowed. "Anatomical!"

It seemed to me that Long Fellow's thoughts were a bit muddled, but he was continuing and the poem was becoming more raunchy with every line. Some four letter words crept in, evoking gasps from the rear. The Silver Fun clubber behind me was asking his wife when the Indian piece would start and was not listening to the poem, which was still in progress. I could see Poppy in the front row, wiggling uneasily. I wondered what she had expected. Poppy is sweet but not really with it.

Herm had had enough. He grabbed my hand and pulled me out to the aisle. I was surprised to see that the Fun Clubbers were all staying but realized they were probably at the mercy of a bus schedule. Some of them were asleep anyway.

Poppy called me that evening. She sounded disconsolate.

"I'm afraid we didn't make nearly enough money," she said. "We took in seventy-five dollars and out of that we have to pay twenty-five dollars for renting the church and four dollars for printing the posters. That leaves us with forty-six dollars, which isn't enough to do any good."

"Maybe you should have charged more for the tickets."

"Then nobody would have come. It's no use. I guess this is the end of The Doghouse. The committee is absolutely crushed."

There was nothing I could say to comfort her. Our local newspaper had refused to send a reporter or reviewer, on the grounds that with the primary election coming up in a few days, they needed all their space for political news and advertising. The benefit, it seemed, was not only mismanaged but ill-timed.

Gloom prevailed until the day after the election. The big issue was a proposal that would drastically reduce taxes. Its passage, by an overwhelming vote, put an end to the plans for renovating the downtown, and The Doghouse was saved.

Poppy told me that they were going to use the forty-six dollars to buy paint to refurbish the place, both inside and out, setting a good example to neighboring businesses, which might follow suit.

"You know that man sitting behind you with the Fun Club?" she said. "Well, he's Mrs. Paterson's father and afterward he called her and complained that he had gone to the benefit expecting to hear a recitation of 'Hiawatha' and he felt cheated and blamed it on her."

"Ah well," I said, "you know what Lincoln said about fooling some of the people."

I didn't tell Poppy, but I do feel just a little guilty about that poster.

20

Sandwich-Board People

I was never one of those people who return from a sale with armloads of fabulous bargains. It was always my destiny to find nothing but useless ugly items that were on sale because no one wanted them. So I stopped going to sales and the quality of my life improved. But the other day I just happened to be walking through Hamilton's linen department on my way out of the store, and there were these irresistible designer towels on sale.

When I saw them I knew they would make Herm's bathroom look like a picture in *House Beautiful*. They were thick and handsome, in deep colors, with the designer's name, Pucci, on the border in bold black letters two inches high. In my mind I saw them replacing the nondescript towels now in use. I pictured Herm looking at them with approval and satisfaction, enjoying the touch of luxury. I bought two sets and hurried home, whipped the old towels off the bar, hung the new ones on, and waited for Herm to find them and express delight.

I was preparing the cocktail tray when he came into the kitchen, looking annoyed.

"Where did those towels come from, Lydia?" he said. "Some Italian hotel?"

"Of course not," I said. "They were marked down to a ridiculous price and I thought they would enhance the glamour of your bath."

"What is Pucky? Or should I say, who?"

"The designer. You should say Poochy. In Italian, *c* before *e* or *i* is pronounced *ch*."

"Why do we need Italian towels?" Herm said. "What's wrong with plain American towels?"

Herm is very patriotic.

"These *are* American," I said. "But it's fashionable now to have designers' names on things— clothes, cars, furniture, linens. It's what rich people have."

"I don't like it," Herm said. "Why should we advertise for this fellow Pucci? I never heard of him. It's a racket, to lure foolish women into spending money."

I was disappointed in Herm's reaction. Probably he had found a worm on one of his new Tiffany roses and it had eaten into his normal good humor.

"I thought you'd like them," I said, carrying the tray out to the balcony.

Herm followed along glumly.

"Women are just a bunch of sheep," he said. "Put up a sign that says Sale and they'll crowd around to buy yesterday's garbage. You'd better take them back."

"I can't. All sales are final on marked-down items."

"Well then, use them in your own bath."

"I can't do that either. They're the wrong color."

It was an impasse.

"Oh, Herm," I said, "I really thought you'd like them because they're so elegant, just like you."

"Well. Uh. I suppose if you can't take them back I can hang them with the name against the wall."

We sat on the balcony with our drinks and the evening paper. I noticed that La Mode de Paris was featuring dresses from "the atelier of Countess Myrtille," and suspected that the countess was really a Seventh Avenue manufacturer with, perhaps, a plump wife named Myrtle. It was an important selling point for Countess Myrtille that all her dresses were distinguished by a little *M* embroidered on a tab that hung over the shoulder like an epaulet. We are becoming a nation of sandwich-board people, I thought. And I'm as bad as the rest, as bad as Mrs. Barnes, a woman I encountered not long ago at a morning coffee.

She had just come from Hamilton's where she had bought some Dior shorts for her father, a blind old man in a nursing home. She opened the package to show us.

"Dad asked me to get him some new underwear," she said. "Aren't these super?"

"Your father wouldn't care if they are Dior or Woolworth's," said the hostess, who knew Mrs. Barnes's father. "You should have bought him ordinary ones and used the extra money to get something he could enjoy. A bunch of flowers that smelled nice, for example."

Mrs. Barnes bristled.

"I want my father to have the best," she said.

But everyone knew that she had bought them to please herself, not her father, who had probably never heard of Dior anyway.

Herm handed me a section of the newspaper.

"Supermarket ads," he said. "Tomorrow's Thursday. There's a special on canned dog food. The dog food with clout, it says here."

I gave him a dirty look.

"The dog on the label," Herm said, rattling the paper to keep my attention, "is by Salvador Dali. You'll want some."

We don't have a dog.

"Keep that up and you'll get it for dinner tomorrow," I told him.

But he was laughing.

We were a little later than usual getting started the next morning and found the parking lot at the market crowded. A Lincoln Continental half a mile long was slanted across two spaces and sticking out into the driving lane. I try to ignore such things, especially since Fred Tucker at the gas station told me about the blood pressure lecture he had been to, but it is hard not to feel indignant about such flagrant disregard for the rights of others.

We found a vacant space a bit farther along and pulled into it. As we walked back, the owners of the Lincoln were climbing out. The driver was a smartly dressed older woman with clean features and smooth skin, the kind of arrogant good looks peculiar to the well-heeled. She had gray eyes, like stones in winter. Her husband was fine-boned and frail. He carried a cane and looked as though he really should be at home with a rug over his knees.

The woman started toward the market, turning to say, "Come *on*, you're so slow. Do you want to wait in the car?"

The words, carelessly tossed, fell between them.

"I'm coming, my dear," said the husband, and he hurried after her.

We went inside. Herm took a cart and I fished out my shopping list and coupons.

We were nearly finished when I picked up a ten-pound sack of potatoes, turned to put it in the cart, and discovered that Herm, as often happens, had vanished. I guessed that he had stopped at the dairy counter to choose a new flavor of yogurt, which he eats privately in the belief that it is healthful. He eats it privately because I can't bear to look at it.

As I stood there clutching the potatoes I saw the rich couple approaching. It was hard to tell if the husband was pushing the cart or leaning on it. The cart was full of goodies—jumbo olives, fresh asparagus, lamb chops, and strawberries. For a moment I felt like the little match girl. But only for a moment.

Near the end of the produce department was a display of potted orchids, green cymbidiums, their splendor unaffected by the cabbages and beans surrounding them. The old man stopped and looked at the orchids with pleasure. He pulled one forward on the shelf and called to his wife.

"Eunice, look here. I'll get you one of these, shall I?"

She turned from pinching some fruit and

flicked her eyes in bored annoyance over the orchid. Not bothering to answer, she merely shook her head and turned away. The eagerness drained from the old man's face and for a moment I thought he was going to cry, but he tightened his mouth, pushed the orchid back, and stood, supported by the cart, waiting.

Herm had come along during this scene. I put the potatoes into the cart and said, "Look, Herm, her dress is R-I-C-C-I, Ritchy, and her bag is G-U-C-C-I, Goochy. I can see the labels."

"Maybe so," Herm said. "But you don't need a label to see that the rest of her is B-I-C-C-I, pronounced—"

"Yes," I said. "Yes indeed."

21

Mrs. Meticulous and the Gray Woman

You would think that with two cars in the family, we would never be without at least one in the carport, but Herm had lent *his* car to his son Mike, whose minibus had broken down, and I had to leave my little two-seater for servicing, so there we were. It is true that we go for long walks every day, but we always drive to some starting-off point.

Herm decided to walk anyway, starting from our house and just going around the neighborhood. I begged off, with the excuse that I had to finish a painting for an art class assignment. It was a fine day, and Herm set off down the hill, resolutely refusing to face the fact that to get back home he would have to walk *up* the hill.

"Be careful not to leave footmarks on Mrs. Meticulous's sidewalk," I told him. "She'll hit you with her broom."

Mrs. Meticulous (my name for her) lives at the corner of Via La Loma, which winds down the hill, and Linda Lane, which, probably because of its proximity to a main thoroughfare, tends to be a bit seedy. Except, that is, for Mrs. Meticulous's corner.

My attention was first drawn to it by an urn that stood three feet high near her house and contained a plant that draped gracefully over the sides and produced flowers of a shade of blue I had never before seen. I pointed it out to Herm, the gardener in our family, and asked him to identify it. As we could not get close to it but observed it only from the car, it was months before we discovered that it was plastic.

Aside from the artificial plant, though, Mrs. M's property was not unattractive. She had a neat bungalow with a two-car garage attached at the side, and several low buildings with apartments and carports, painted white with green trim, surrounded by tiny lawns, miniature flower beds, and white picket fences. The tenants of the apartments, whom we occasionally spotted when driving past, were mostly older women who collaborated with Mrs. M in keeping the premises immaculate, and who, I suspected, would be summarily asked to move if they became incapable of sweeping their sidewalks and weeding their own little flower beds. Needless to say, no dogs or cats were permitted. I wondered if perhaps some of the tenants indulged in a hidden canary or a wee bowl of goldfish.

Whenever we saw Mrs. M herself, she was busy doing something to further perfect her property. We could see her up on a ladder scrubbing the top side of her aluminum awning with a long-handled brush, or polishing her already gleaming door handle, or scooping the grass cuttings into a bag. One day we saw her squatting in the gutter with a brush and dustpan, gathering whatever bits of debris had collected there.

Herm professed to admire all this.

"She certainly keeps that place looking nice," he said.

"The woman is a fanatic," I said.

But it bothered me, just a little, whenever I saw Mrs. M. The fact is, I would much rather paint a picture than scrub the floor, and sometimes the floor shows it.

Once Herm said, "You know what, Lydia, ha ha, I can write with my finger on my desk top. Ha ha."

I found a dustcloth and handed it to him.

"Have a go at it, there's a good chap," I said cheerfully, doing my imitation of the phony Englishmen who sell men's discount clothing on television.

He backed away, startled. I wondered if I should feel guilty but decided not to. There was no further mention of dust.

Fanatic or not, Mrs. Meticulous fascinates me. She is not tall, but powerfully built, with broad shoulders and an American Gothic face, only rounder. Her long, dark hair is always pulled back severely into a knot. I suppose sometimes she gets dressed up and goes out, but I have seen her only in her working clothes, dark slacks and plain blouses, endlessly sweeping. When she is not in view as we pass her house, I feel sure she is inside, chasing dirt, chanting "Spit and polish, spit and polish, I will all the dirt abolish."

Next door to Mrs. M, on the uphill side of Via La Loma, lived the Gray Woman and her little gray poodle. Everything about the Gray Woman was gray and sad looking; the peeling shreds of paint on her run-down cottage; the two-foot-high weeds in her untended garden, surrounded by a sagging chicken-wire fence; her own thick body always wrapped in an old gray bathrobe, tied around the middle with a frayed cord; her lined gray face, sagging like her fence, topped by tousled gray hair. Every morning between nine and ten the Gray Woman would stand for a while on her front porch, leaning on the broken railing, smoking, while the poodle rummaged in the weeds. She would gaze into space, peering up the hill or out at the street. She never turned her head in the direction of Mrs. M's sparkling establishment.

Although I disliked Mrs. M for being such a perfect housekeeper, I did pity her, living next door to the only piggy place on the entire block.

On the day Herm walked down the hill, he returned, as he had promised, in time for lunch.

"I had a little chat with Mrs. Meticulous," he informed me, as we sat down to leftover reheated Sauté de Veau Marengo.

"She really is a lovely woman," said Herm.

"Oh she is, is she?"

"She was setting out some marigolds just inside her fence when I went by and I said, What a nice place you have here, or something like that, so she stood up and talked to me. Very pleasant."

"Um," I said.

"You always say she looks so grim."

"Uh huh."

"I said it was a shame her neighbors were so untidy, meaning, of course, the Gray Woman."

"And what did she say?"

"She said, 'That woman is my sister and she lives like that, with her filthy dog, to spite me. Only to spite me. For ten years now!' "

He paused for a forkful.

"Umm. This is *good* stew, Sugar."

"Then what?"

"Nothing. But she did look grim, as you say, when she spoke of the Gray Woman."

"Did she say why?"

"No, and I didn't feel I could ask her. Besides, I was getting hungry."

I was, of course, intrigued by the drama being played on Via La Loma. I marveled at the cleverness of the Gray Woman in devising such a fiendish revenge and wondered what Mrs. M had done to bring it upon herself, if, indeed, it was a deliberate action. Perhaps it was only the old banal story of two women wanting the same man and Mrs. M had won. More likely, I thought, Mrs. Meticulous, in addition to being a compulsive cleaner, has a streak of paranoia and suspects persecution where none exists.

One morning, leaving Herm happily digging in his rose bed, I went out to do a few errands. As I drove down the hill, I saw the Gray Woman leaning as usual on the porch railing, gazing blankly at the street. Just beyond, I could see the ample backside of Mrs. M as she searched the grass between the sidewalk and the street, looking for nonexistent weeds. She was brandishing a notched weeding stick and looked determined.

Everything happened very fast. As I came

opposite the Gray Woman's house, with a tailgater just behind me, the poodle, finding the
gate accidentally unlatched, dashed out in fierce
attack upon my wheels, yipping and jigging until the wheel hit him, thud!, and he bounced
back and lay still. Mrs. M dropped her weeder
and sprang out into the street, where she gathered up the dog and stood holding him in her
arms like a baby. I pulled over to the curb and
stopped. The tailgater, a person of indetermi-
nate sex, honked angrily and sped on. The Gray
Woman stepped down from her porch and advanced upon the scene, walking, in grimy felt
slippers, as though she had two wooden legs
and faulty balance.

I was close enough to Mrs. M to hear her
mutter "Drunk again," and as the Gray Woman
approached it became quite evident that she had
indeed been hitting the early morning bottle.

"Is he dead?" I said to Mrs. M.

She shook her head.

"No. Stunned, I think. Broken leg, maybe."

She handed him to the Gray Woman, and
said, "Just a minute, I'll get my purse," and she
rushed into her house and out again, locking
her door as she left.

She climbed into the tiny back of my car, not
really a proper seat at all; the Gray Woman sat
in front with the dog. He was really a wretched-

looking dog, as uncared for as his owner. I could not help thinking that it might be just as well if he died and left what must surely be a miserable existence.

We started off to the animal hospital. Up to this moment the Gray Woman had not uttered a sound, but suddenly tears began to trickle down her face and in a hoarse voice but with a flawless accent, she said,

"Ah, Jean-Claude, Jean-Claude! Mon pauvre p'tit!"

The dog whimpered a bit in response to this, but otherwise there was silence until I parked in front of the First Street Pet Hospital. We all trooped in, the Gray Woman carrying the dog in front of her like an offering, then Mrs. M, and I gloomily trailing after them.

When we entered the imitation-wood waiting room, the only occupant was a girl with a scarf tied fashionably around her head, covering her eyebrows, an unbecoming arrangement, in my opinion. She was holding, on a leash, a handsome Irish setter which had evidently not been bathed for many weeks, and reeked of dogginess in an unpleasant way. The sound of continual but routine barking came through a side door leading to the area where animals were boarded.

Mrs. M went to the counter and, gesturing to the Gray Woman and the poodle, explained that we had an emergency. A girl came from behind the counter and led them to the rear. Convinced that three, at any time, is a crowd, I stayed behind, shivering in a corner and wondering what would happen to Jean-Claude.

A man in paint-stained overalls came in with a nervous collie, which kept straining at the leash, trying to get to the door and escape, sitting up on her hind legs and begging piteously for release. Her name was Genevieve and she was to spend the weekend being boarded, clearly against her wishes.

If Jean-Claude should die now, how would the Gray Woman take it?

The setter, named Ollie, was escorted to the back for rabies and distemper shots. Once he had gone, we could enjoy breathing again. I hoped the doctor would tell Ollie's owner to bathe him, poor creature.

I kept wondering what they were doing to Jean-Claude.

An excited woman in a white wig came in and explained that she had that morning knocked over the bottle of dog medicine and had come for more.

"So upset I put on different colored socks," she told the girl.

I looked, and sure enough, one blue and one brown.

The medicine was produced, six dollars please, and as the woman fished out her money, she said that the dog was doing very well now.

"If I can prolong his life . . . ," she finished, sounding almost tearful.

I was sure that Jean-Claude had died and they were all back there burying him.

Finally Mrs. M and the Gray Woman reappeared, Jean-Claude in the Gray Woman's arms. He had one leg tied to his body with a bandage that went clear around him. He would have to walk on three legs for a while.

"Dislocated hip," Mrs. M said. "He'll be okay."

She paid the bill. The Gray Woman, in her bathrobe, obviously had no money with her.

We all got back in the car and I drove them home.

"I'm sorry," I said to the Gray Woman, as she got out. "I hope he'll be all right now."

"Thank you," she said, in her low growly voice. "It wasn't your fault. I know that."

It was getting late and I was too unnerved to do the errands I had planned. I drove up the hill and told Herm all about it. He sat patiently on a sack of fertilizer and let me go on.

"Perhaps now they'll be reconciled," I ended.

Herm says I have a naively optimistic outlook.

It would have been, of course, a storybook ending, but life is not like a storybook.

A few months later Herm and I were having our predinner drink and sharing the evening paper when my attention was caught by an address in the obituary column. (Because I have always been fascinated by people's houses, I remember their addresses rather than their names). The item said that Mrs. Martha Webb Abernethy, of 303 Via La Loma, had died after a short illness. It said she was born in Danville, Illinois; had been an actress in the thirties, under the name of Martha Webb; had lived abroad for many years; and was survived by her sister, Mrs. Gertrude Weber Abernethy, of 301 Via La Loma.

"Herm! Listen to this!"

Herm tore his attention reluctantly from the garden page. I read the item to him.

"It's all there, Herm. It explains everything. The Gray Woman, poor thing, was an actress, married to Mr. Abernethy, and probably she was more interested in her career than in a pleasant home life (look at her house!), which is what he wanted. A simple fellow, very likely."

"What's wrong with wanting a pleasant home life?" Herm demanded.

I was not about to be drawn into one of those pointless women's lib discussions. I know what I know and I felt sorry for the Gray Woman.

"So Mr. Abernethy divorced her and married

her sister Mrs. Meticulous, and the Gray Woman went to France with a broken heart, and came back after Mr. Abernethy died, to punish her sister. So it was not, after all, paranoia on Mrs. M's part."

"You're building a skyscraper with no foundation," Herm said. "Just because they were both Mrs. Abernethy. They might have married brothers, or cousins with the same name."

I looked at the clock and realized that something was about to boil over in the kitchen. Anyway, it was all there, really, in that one short paragraph, Herm's objections notwithstanding.

Jean-Claude, fully recovered and exquisitely groomed, now lives with Mrs. Meticulous. She built a neat dog run for him beside her house, and planted purple clematis vines to grow up the sides and shield it from the street.

"I told you she was a lovely woman," Herm said, smugly, as though it were all his doing.

If I were given to violence, I would have thrown something at him.

22

Don't Play It Again, Jasper

Secret recipes are, of course, essential to the business success of professional chefs and food purveyors, but I thought it was just plain silly for my friend Dulcie (short for Dulcinea), to refuse to share her grandmother's recipe for beaten biscuits. Dulcie was born and raised in South Carolina, and her biscuits are genuine.

"I thought it would be so nice to have them when the children come for Christmas," I said to Herm.

We were having our predinner cocktail on the balcony and I was thinking about food because it was almost time to go in and start cooking.

"You can't really expect her to share her only treasure, Lydia," Herm said. "You have so many, but poor Dulcie—"

"What do you mean, I have so many?"

"Well, you have your painting talent, and you have me—"

Herm would never make it as a stand-up comedian, but that's all right with me. I'd hate to live with a man who was always being funny.

Nothing more was said about the biscuits, but by some sort of ESP Dulcie must have known I was still hankering for the recipe. She phoned the very next morning.

"I've been thinking about it," she said, "and I finally decided that Grandmother wouldn't mind if I gave you the recipe."

"Oh Dulcie, that's wonderful."

"Hy-ever," she said, "hy-ever, I wondered if in return you would do something for me."

"If you want that little painting I did of your house, I was planning to give it to you for Christmas."

"That would be lovely, but what I was going to ask was, would you come over and talk to Jasper. He's having some sort of crisis. About his job."

"What seems to be the trouble?"

"He wants to quit and do something entirely different. Like deep-sea fishing or selling ice cream from a wagon."

"Sounds rather impractical," I said.

"He's been living on tranquilizers for months now," Dulcie said.

I should explain that after Jasper retired from being a school administrator in Iowa, he came to California and got a part-time job with a classical music radio station. It is he who selects the records to be played day and night, interrupted only by news on the hour and commercial messages.

"He won't listen to me," Dulcie said, "but I know he admires you and maybe you could talk some sense into him."

"I'll be right over," I said.

Dulcie was in the garden pulling up weeds when I arrived. She has the southern woman's knack of looking smart and pretty even in gardening clothes and no makeup. It would be easy to hate her for that but I decided not to, because of the biscuits. I noted that the Charlotte Armstrong that Herm had given her when he dug it up to make space for Mr. Lincoln was doing well and knew he would be pleased to hear about it.

"Just go on in," she said.

I found Jasper slumped on the living room sofa, dejectedly staring at his shoes. Beside him on the blue upholstery was a scattering of papers. He looked up when I came in.

"Hullo," he said. "Did Dulcie tell you that I'm going to resign?"

"But why, Jasper?" I said. "For a music lover like yourself, it's a perfect job."

He picked up a handful of papers and waved them at me.

"See this? These are all letters from people who hate me. Mostly women. But this one is from a man blaming me for his divorce."

"Why Jasper! I thought you and Dulcie—"

"No no. It was because his wife got so depressed listening to the Tchaikovsky Sixth while she was cooking dinner that she threw all the food into the sink and drank half a bottle of Scotch. They had a big fight and one thing led to another. He says it's my fault."

"In a way it is," I said. "I tend to react the same way to the Tchaikovsky Sixth. Have you ever done any cooking?"

"No," Jasper said. "If I had to cook for myself I'd eat out or live on cornflakes."

"What about the other letters?"

"They're almost all from people who object to the programming between five and six. They say that's the most important time of the day, musically speaking, and what they hear on the radio will determine what the family gets for dinner. Listen to this one."

He shuffled through the papers and found one on pink stationery.

" 'Dear Jasper Hooton, I sure wish you'd lose that recording of *Til Eulenspiegel*. It makes me so nervous that last night I dropped an egg on the floor, on the new kitchen carpet. If you had had to clean it up you would be more careful about what you play!' "

"Surely you get letters of thanks, too."

"Well, there's this one. 'Dear Sir, Leslie and I sure do thank you for playing our song last night at five-thirty. It was our twentieth anniversary. How did you know?' "

"That's very nice, Jasper. What was it you played for them?"

"I figured out that must have been the day I played the Tchaikovsky Sixth. I had a lot of letters about it. People react to it in various ways."

"Evidently."

I wondered what kind of people could think of the Tchaikovsky Sixth as "our song." Probably the same ones who flock to four-handkerchief movies because they love to suffer.

"Here's another," Jasper said. " 'Jasper Hooton you creep!' I don't think that's very nice, do you, Lydia? 'My husband is on a low-cholesterol diet but all that Beethoven makes me put everything into cream sauces. If my husband drops dead, it will be your fault.' "

"Oh dear," I said.

"You see, the trouble is that people mostly don't write at all when they're satisfied. Only when they have complaints."

"It's very hard," I said.

"Listen to this one. 'Dear Mr. Hooton, I wish you would not play any more Mendelssohn for a while. I have an irresistible impulse to make chicken salad whenever I hear Mendelssohn and my family is getting tired of cold meals.' Or this. 'That Schubert chamber music always makes me cry, so I can't see what I am doing. Last night I put in too much salt and ruined a big pot of stew. With the price of groceries today . . .' And so on. I can't stand it any more."

I sat down beside him on the sofa and patted his hand.

"Jasper, you must see this as a real challenge. After all, you're the one in charge. You have tremendous power for influencing people. You might change the course of history."

He looked at me with bloodshot eyes.

"What can I do?" he said.

"First you must make a list of the records that the cooks object to and schedule them for three A.M. or some such time. Then you should concentrate, for a while at least, on Mozart, Vivaldi, and Pergolesi during the cooking hour. Anyone who objects to that can be ignored as a person not in possession of his senses."

I stood up and prepared to leave.

"Now buck up, Jasper. Everything's going to be fine."

At the door I had a sudden thought.

"Just one thing," I said, "you know that Mozart piano piece you sometimes play, that Rondo in A Minor. I had to study it as a child with a teacher I hated, and it upsets me so much to hear it that the other night all I could fix for dinner was martinis and peanut butter sandwiches. It was all your fault."

Jasper groaned and buried his face in his hands.

"You can stop worrying about Jasper now, Dulcie," I said as I went through the garden. "He's all straightened out, I think."

She fished in her pocket and handed me a folded paper as though it were the Kohinoor diamond.

"Oh, I do hope so," she said. "I'm really grateful. And when you make the biscuits, remember that you must beat them by hand for exactly forty-seven minutes or they won't be any good."

23

Stars of the Morning

One of the streets Herm and I particularly favor for our daily walk is Flower Street, because it is lined with well-kept houses that I enjoy looking at, and well-kept gardens that Herm inspects with interest. But as in any neighborhood, there are always a few places that have been allowed to become shabby. One of these was on the corner of Flower Street and Via Halcón, so named because an early settler had seen a hawk there, or thought he had.

It was a large square Victorian house, with porches, balconies, bay windows, and a charming cupola. Weatherbeaten paint, relinquishing its hold on the clapboard siding, shed mournful gray flakes that drifted over the weedy lawn, where two bad-tempered dogs patrolled the premises behind a wrought-iron fence. On the mansard roof, the shingles were curled and split.

The most infallible symbol of decline, a tipsy shutter dangling by one hinge, hung in plain sight on the front façade. The only cheerful feature of the place was a weathervane on the cupola. It was a wrought-iron fish that no longer swam in the direction of the wind but had become fixed with its nose pointed forever south, toward the ocean. This seemed to us completely appropriate.

It was exactly the sort of house to appeal to Mr. Northrop, an enterprising real estate broker who bought crumbling houses in good neighborhoods, renovated them from top to bottom, and then sold them for fantastic prices. He was able to do this because he had excellent taste and plenty of capital. When Mr. Northrop finished with a house and planted his discreet For Sale sign in the lawn, I liked to steer Herm in its direction so that I could stand in front of it, drooling, for a few minutes.

There was nothing to indicate that the house on Flower Street had changed hands until one day we noticed that the occupants and their dogs were gone, and Mr. Northrop's crew had taken over. For weeks they swarmed through the property and when they had finished, it was as elegant a mansion as could be found anywhere, although the weathervane had proved impossible to repair and the fish continued its hopeless journey to the ocean. But real estate prices had been rising steadily, and there were not many rich people who wanted such a big old-fashioned house. The For Sale sign remained in the lawn. Mr. Northrop paid the taxes and kept the lawn mowed. We were sure he was getting discouraged.

One day as we walked up Flower Street we encountered unusual activity around the house with the fish. Three huge vans were parked at the curb and two more in the next block. Men scurried back and forth dragging elaborate equipment, some of which was taken into the house and some set up on the lawn. Curtains had been hung on the front windows. From the nature of the equipment, and the sight of three folding canvas armchairs, occupied by magisterial individuals whose duties were clearly supervisory, Herm and I inferred that a movie was being made. This happened fairly often in Los Barcos, and the evening paper generally made reference to it, naming the famous stars who could have been seen emoting in the middle of one of our streets, and inevitably drawing angry comment in the Letters to the Editor column from citizens who objected to the public streets being blocked off for the benefit of a movie company.

Herm and I had not been to the movies for

several years. Herm refused to go any more when it became clear that no matter what the movie was about, there would be scenes of naked people bouncing under the covers. Herm considered this an invasion of privacy, pointing out that although doing it is fun, watching other people doing it is distasteful. Herm is not prudish, but he has definite ideas about decorum.

"Let's just watch for a few minutes," I pleaded. "It's as close as I ever get to the movies nowadays."

"I thought we were out for exercise," Herm said.

"Maybe that actress you saw on the *Today* show will be in it," I said. "The one with all the cleavage."

"Not likely," Herm said, but he looked faintly interested.

"She's just the type for a period movie," I said, pressing my advantage. "I'll bet any minute now she will come through the front door in one of those low-cut costumes with a cinched-in waist and a bustle."

"You're piling it on too thick, Lydia, but okay, we'll watch for a minute."

Ladders, cameras, lights, and miles of wire were carried out of the trailers and in through the iron gate at the corner of the property, where a city policeman was stationed, presumably to keep the movie stars from being mobbed by fans. None of the bystanders, however, looked dangerous. They were mostly the retired people who lived in the neighborhood and were out for their morning stroll. About a dozen were lined up along the fence on the Via Halcón side, which was sunny. As some drifted away, others arrived.

"Well, this should help Northrop with his expenses," Herm remarked.

Except for his faith in seed catalog pictures, Herm is really a hardheaded fellow.

An elderly woman, leaning heavily on the arm of a nurse-attendant, tottered up to the fence and held on to the bars. She wore a gray hat with a long drooping feather that kept floating into the nurse's face.

"I think we've got your hat on wrong," the nurse said in a concerned voice.

She removed the hat, turned it around so that the feather was on the other side, and set it back firmly.

"Thank you, dear," the old woman said.

The hat was now on back to front, but nobody seemed to notice.

A portly man with an overweight basset hound came puffing along. The man stopped to look and the hound, glad of a chance to rest, lay down on the sidewalk, wheezing on my feet. I moved away a few steps. We were joined by a pretend rancher in an ankle-length tweed coat and a cowboy hat.

Inside the fence, the people bustling about were not exciting to look at. They were, in fact, the most ordinary-looking people I had seen in a long time. In Los Barcos, where eccentric dress is the norm, it was strange to see this company in plain jeans and undecorated T-shirts, calmly going about their business. But we knew they were merely the stagehands, preparing for the entrance of the stars.

A thump thump heralded the approach of the woman with three legs, who lived nearby. We had often seen her before. I was convinced that she was the retired headmistress of an English girls' school, a woman of great dignity and forceful personality. She always wore a green tweed suit, and her third leg, which was a crutch disguised in a casing of plaster to resemble a leg, was dressed to match, in green tweed and with a shoe matching the ones on her real feet. Nobody paid much attention to her. They were all concentrating on the activity inside the fence.

Coming toward us from across Via Halcón was another familiar neighborhood figure, the sensitive-nose woman. She was thin and sour, and when she passed anyone in the street, she always looked straight at him and said "You stink" with a depth of feeling that left the accused person feeling worried, at the very least.

The suspense built slowly. We watched men climb up on ladders, and down again. With unwavering attention, we followed the wires being snaked around and I wondered how soon someone would trip over them. An enormous arc light on top of a ladder was turned on and pointed into a window of the house. From the position and shape of the window, I deduced it was a powder room or a coat closet beside the front door, and concluded that they were making a mystery movie and someone would discover a body in the closet.

Patiently we waited for the appearance of the stars, and the moment when one of the directors in a canvas chair would shout "Lights! Camera! Action!" or "Take One!" Nothing happened. The elderly woman grew tired of hanging on to the fence and was led away by her companion. The portly man pulled his hound to its feet and they went on, snuffling and puffing.

"Come on, Lydia," Herm said. "We can't stand here all day."

He forced the issue by moving purposefully toward the corner. I would have liked to wait longer to see the drama that was about to take place but loyally followed Herm. I couldn't go, however, until I had found out what I would be missing. We approached the policeman.

"Do you know who the stars in this movie are?" I said.

He was pleased to be asked, to justify his being there by at least answering questions, since clearly he would not be called upon to restrain a mob.

"Stars?" he said.

He pointed to one of the undistinguished-looking people on the lawn.

"See that man? He plays the father. That's the main part. They're making a commercial for Kentucky Fried Chicken."

"Oh, Herm," I said, disappointed, as we moved away. "All that standing around and I didn't get to see any stars at all."

"Yes you did, Sugar," Herm said.

He indicated, with a slight bob of his head, the woman with three legs, the sensitive-nose woman, the pretend rancher, and a few other exotics who were now lined up along the fence watching the performance.

"They were standing all around you."

24

S.T.O.P.

Herm and I had finished reading the paper and were sitting on the balcony enjoying the view with our predinner cocktails.

"Where I lived in the Midwest," I said, "there wasn't any view, there wasn't any ocean, and the climate was almost too much for human endurance, but I had neighbors all around on whom I could call for help if I was in trouble."

"This just isn't a neighborly place, Sugar," Herm said.

"We could be robbed and murdered and buried in the backyard, and the murderers could move in here and give parties and nobody on this street would even notice."

"California just *is* that way," Herm said. "It's because people come here from all over. They don't have much in common."

"We've lived here seven years now," I said,

"and I still don't know what the people next door look like. All I know is the noise they make."

"Well, we know their dog, Bonnie. Bonnie's okay."

"I don't know which is worse," I said, "that booming rock music or the revolting smell of their barbecues."

"Maybe you ought to go over and ask them not to play the music so loud," Herm said, knowing perfectly well that I'm as unlikely as he is ever to do such a thing.

"I keep thinking maybe they'll move away," I said.

"You've been saying that for six years, ever since they moved in."

"It's too bad the hedge is so high," I said. "I'd like to know what they look like just so I could cut them dead if I met them in the street."

"Surely you don't object to the McVittys, Lydia. They're good neighbors."

"Yes, but look at us, sandwiched between the McVittys, who are too tottery to chase burglars, and the rock music-barbecue people, who are antisocial. It gives me an uneasy feeling."

I picked up the newspaper.

"There were nine burglaries yesterday on this side of town. There was one just over in the next block."

"Uh," Herm said.

He had just discovered a new garden catalog in his pocket and his attention was concentrated on a description of rutabagas, which we could not grow here anyway. If the house started to burn down while Herm was reading the paper or a garden catalog, I suspect he would finish reading before calling the fire department. In fact, he wouldn't even notice that the house was burning down.

I decided to wait for a more propitious moment.

That night, at two A.M., I was awakened by mysterious sounds from the patio. I turned on the light and shook Herm.

"Burglars," I said. "Trying to break in the kitchen door."

"Your imagination," Herm said, and pulled the covers over his head.

The noise was repeated, a sort of rattle bang clunk.

"There it goes again," I said. "Herm, I'm scared."

He got up to investigate while I held the telephone, one finger already on button 9 to call the police.

"Your burglar was Snowfoot," he reported when he came back. "He was after that sardine can in the garbage."

Snowfoot, the Gudges' white-footed black cat,

does not stay at home where he belongs—and who can blame him, the Gudges being what they are. He spends most of his time in our garden, on the prowl. Our garbage can is kept in a fenced enclosure, which we thought would make it inaccessible to animals, but we had underestimated Snowfoot.

"Last night it was Snowfoot. Tonight it might be a real burglar," I said the next morning at breakfast. "I think we should get a burglar alarm system."

"Nonsense," Herm said.

"Good. I'll get after it right away," I said, and consulted the Yellow Pages.

Several companies sent men to give us estimates. As they snooped through our house I worried that they might themselves be burglars, using this method to "case the joint," as I believe they say in criminal circles. However, it was a chance we had to take. We signed a contract with S.T.O.P.

The person in charge of the S.T.O.P. installation was Warren, a handsome fellow with the stalwart appearance of a movie police hero. After our first meeting with Warren I already felt protected.

Warren immediately slapped his company's decals on strategic doors and windows. The decals read:

S.T.O.P.
Security Tested Owners Protection
Alarm System

"Just seeing these will deter most burglars," he said.

Then he backed up his car in an effort to turn it around at the end of our driveway, and as I stood there making frantic but useless signals, he drove it straight into an enormous potted yucca at the corner of the house. It made me wonder if Warren was really as competent as he looked.

He apologized, picked up the pieces, and promised to pay for a new pot and do the re-planting himself. I spent two days driving around town trying to find a pot of the proper size, an activity that kept me too busy to worry about burglars and, because of its connection with S.T.O.P., also made me feel more secure.

On Wednesday, the day the alarm was to be installed, I awoke early, with a vaguely sick feeling. Breakfast will help, I decided, and went to the kitchen. Herm was still asleep. I ate my usual boiled egg, toast, and coffee. Then I stood up and had to grab the table to keep from keeling over. I knew immediately what it was—"that thing that's going around." I staggered back to bed and stayed there two days, while the

S.T.O.P. crew, directed by Warren, swarmed through the house, drilling, pounding, sawing, shouting to each other and trailing miles of wire behind them.

Whenever a decision had to be made, about where to put a switch, for example, or how far would we want to keep a window open, Herm referred them to me because, as he said, it was *my* project.

"Sorry to disturb you, lady," Sonny, the big fat one, would say, "but we have to know—"

I would open one eye and give him the answer. I must say they were all very sympathetic and tried to keep the racket to a minimum when they were in the bedroom. Through it all, Herm hovered, brought me cups of tea, speculated gloomily on what dreadful ailment might have struck me down (he was not altogether convinced that it was "the thing that's going around"), and remarked from time to time that it might be less trouble to have an occasional burglar than to go through this. But he was careful to add "Ha ha" when he said that.

By Friday evening the S.T.O.P. alarm was installed. I was back on my feet though still weak and slow-witted. Herm had feared a tangle of wires draped everywhere but with great skill they had managed to conceal the wires, and except for the decals and a few switches and boxes sprouting on the house, there was no visible evidence of the elaborate layout that now protected us.

Warren gave us instruction on its use. First, we had to make sure all the doors and windows were properly closed. If they were, the green light would be glowing. Then we could "arm the system," as Warren expressed it, by pushing a button inside the house or by turning a key on the outside. That would turn off the green light and turn on the red light.

"If you've been out," Warren cautioned, "remember to turn off the alarm when you come back, *before* you open the door. Or else all hell's gonna break loose."

We promised to be careful. Warren backed his car down the driveway and disappeared.

"Come on, Sugar. I'll take you out to dinner. You're not up to cooking yet," Herm said.

I accepted with gratitude. We decided to go to a new Chinese place where the cook speaks no English, only Chinese, and you have to order the food by number from the menu. He has memorized the numbers—14 is beef with pea pods, 23 is shrimp with almonds, and so on. He is an excellent cook.

"Now for the countdown," Herm said, as he locked the front door. "That was Three. Lock door."

"Two. Check for the green light," I said.

"One. Turn the key to set the alarm. Red light comes on," Herm said.

"Zero. Blast off! Oh, I just realized I forgot to pick up that letter I wanted to mail. Would you let me back in the house, please, sweetie?"

Herm unlocked the door for me and I opened it. All hell broke loose, just as Warren had said it would. It was rather like the clanging in a firehouse when the alarm is sounded. But louder. I know, because I once served on the election board in a firehouse polling place, and every time an alarm came in, all the workers and all the voters would jump up into the air. It was a nervewracking experience. This was worse.

"Turn if off! Turn it off!" I yelled.

Herm turned the key. The clamor did not stop. Inside the house I pushed the control button. Nothing happened. The clanging continued, incessant, earsplitting. I telephoned the S.T.O.P. company, who promised to send someone but said it would take fifteen minutes for him to reach us. In the meantime, they said, we could go to the box in the crawlspace and open it with a special key. They explained where the key was. We would then pull up the lever marked X. That should stop the bell until the repair man could get to the house.

I found Herm in the driveway with a group of

people—old Mr. McVitty from next door, Mr. Gudge from across the street, and two strange men I had never seen before. They looked like possible burglars.

By this time the alarm had been ringing for almost ten minutes. I was beginning to feel faint again. Herm found the box and key and pulled the lever marked X and the noise stopped. But the lever would not stay pulled. The instant Herm took his hand off it, the clangor would start again.

Mr. McVitty, his wispy white hair blowing, stood by, shifting from one foot to the other, asking "What is happening? What is happening?"

Mr. Gudge held back a little—he has not been very friendly since the time we refused to sign his petition—and said sourly, "Them things no good."

One of the strange men stepped forward.

"Pete Bewley, next door," he said, jerking his head toward the rock music-barbecue establishment behind the hedge. "Let me see that."

He looked at Lever X, which Herm was still holding in place, spotted a scrap of wood on a shelf, and shoved it in under the lever to hold it.

"Well! Thank you, Mr. Bewley," Herm said.

Everyone stood around for a minute or two but there was nothing more to be done. I assured them that the repair man was coming, and they dispersed, Bewley and his friend vanishing through a hole in the hedge.

Sonny arrived, poked about for a while, and finally found a short in the system, which he repaired.

Herm locked the door, turned on the red light again, and we went to the Chinese restaurant.

"Now you see, Lydia," Herm said, as we sat in a dark booth enjoying numbers 14 and 23, "our neighbors came right over when we had trouble. And we finally got to meet Bewley, after all this time. He seemed like a decent fellow."

I giggled because I still felt a little weak and silly.

"The thing is," I said, "when Bewley came over I was in the house telephoning and then I was so upset I didn't really look at him. So that now I still wouldn't recognize him if we met."

"Mostly all you could see was the beard," Herm said. "Maybe I should grow one."

"Don't you dare. Anyway, it will probably be another seven years before we see him again."

"Doesn't matter," Herm said. "We know he's there."

25

The Pink House

"**Q**uick, Lydia!" Herm called. "You're on television!"

I dropped everything and rushed in. Herm was laughing so hard that I could hardly hear the commercial. It was for a real estate company in the city, promising that if they are given the job of selling your house, they will bring only bonafide customers to inspect it, no Snoopnoses. They showed an animated cartoon of a group of Snoopnoses, blobby oval creatures with sharp noses and grabby eyes, swarming through a house, opening closets and dresser drawers, peeking in the medicine cabinet, examining the pictures on the walls, and finally swarming out. "The Snoopnoses will not buy your house," a voice warned. "They have come only to pry."

My career as a Snoopnose began when I was nine. Home was a crowded city apartment, where

I had to share a room with my sister. I knew, from reading about it, that there were people who lived in separate houses with gardens. They could open the door and step out onto the grass and not into the hall with a lot of doors leading to other apartments. I knew this but did not really believe it until one Sunday afternoon my father turned up with a new car and took my sister and me for a drive.

He drove us out into a suburban area where I had never been. On a street called Brook Road I saw the Pink House. It was a vision of Paradise.

"That's mine! That's mine!" I shouted.

My sister had to make do with one farther along, not quite so pretty and not even pink.

After that, whenever my father came to take us for a drive, I would ask him to go by way of the Pink House. Sometimes he did. Not always. After he and my mother were divorced, he stopped coming. I did not miss him, but I did miss the Pink House. I've been looking for it ever since. Brook Road is all apartment houses now, so I have been looking elsewhere.

Since that time I have lived in many houses. Herm and I never considered an apartment, because Herm is happiest when on his hands and knees in a garden, and I like the option of being able to play the piano in the middle of the night.

This is something I never do, but I want to know I can if I should ever be in the mood.

Number 10 Rosebush Plaza is just right for us. It gives the illusion of spaciousness by means of an entire wall of glass, opening to a balcony overlooking the city and the ocean. A house with no flaws has never been built, but we found that ours had remarkably few.

When we moved in, Herm thought that would be the end of house-hunting. He didn't realize that I am an incurable housaholic, embarked on an eternal search for the Pink House. Every Sunday afternoon when the Open House signs go up, Herm and I are out there.

We take a list of half a dozen or so, culled from the Sunday real estate pages, and concentrated in a limited area so that we don't have to drive too far. We always see an assortment, handsome façades concealing dismal interiors, and vice versa. The real estate agents are eager, and we don't feel guilty about taking their time because there are seldom other customers about and besides, we are, really, looking for the Pink House, although we never try to explain this. Sometimes, if they are too insistent, we give them phony names.

No, I do not open people's cupboards or touch their possessions. In fact, I much prefer unoccupied houses, where I am spared any feeling of infringing on someone's privacy.

Last Sunday we set out as usual with our list. This is what we saw:

1. A brand-new house full of the intoxicating essence of raw wood, attended by the builder himself, a Mr. Shaw, who expressed delight at the opportunity of showing us through. He had constructed a tiled entry one step higher than the surrounding area, a perfect trap for the unwary, as there was no reason to expect a step in that place. I envisioned people pitching forward with alarming frequency.

"Real Spanish tile," Mr. Shaw said.

A proud smile of achievement lit his big red face as he ushered us from one room to the next.

"What is this alcove for?" I said, as we walked down the hall to the bedrooms.

He shrugged.

"Whatever you like," he said. "I put in special touches like that, all over the house. More expensive. But you can tell this place is custom-built. Not a tract house."

The alcove, one of several, was simply an indentation in the wall, not large enough to hold a piece of furniture, but too large to ignore. It looked as though a giant had leaned against the wall and pushed it in. On the other side, it protruded into a clothes closet, effectively cutting off half the closet from any practical use.

"Hm-m. Very interesting," Herm said.

Mr. Shaw was pleased.

"Look here," he said, guiding us into an enormous bathroom.

He pointed to the pseudo-Moorish lamps, installed in such a way that the chains hung in front of the face of a person looking in the mirror.

"Oh my!" I said. "How unusual."

He wanted approbation.

"I designed it myself," he said. "One of a kind, this house is."

"It's obvious that no expense has been spared," Herm said.

Unlike me, Herm is usually tactful. He seldom lets anger or indignation cause him to blurt out remarks he will later regret. I hope that I will eventually learn from his example.

We thanked Mr. Shaw for letting us see the house and said we were sorry that it was too large for us.

2. A handsome older house, now vacant, on a fashionable street. Inside, grime and ghosts. The ghosts of children riding tricycles up and down the hall on rainy days, of a depressed housewife standing defeated before a greasy stove in a sad, cream-colored kitchen. I could hear spectral rain

spattering against the windows, and the children screeching and banging about in the hall. I could see the woman plainly. She had lank brown hair and an uneven hem on her shapeless dress. I wanted to reach out to her and say "Don't despair. This will pass." Indeed, I had extended my hand to her when I realized that Herm was giving me a funny look.

3. An odd little house, described as an artist's hideaway. An intriguing description, no matter how often I see it in the ads. After all, I consider myself a real artist now, with my collection of canvases piling up against the walls of my studio, a toolshed in the backyard. This house must have been the residence of bookish people who built crude shelves in unlikely corners as their library grew out of bounds. It had charm, but only one bathroom, and a great deal of I-did-it-myself carpentry. One felt that much of it would collapse when the thumbtacks fell out.

4. A bungalow, dating from the twenties, on a street lined with similar bungalows. It had a front porch, with the hooks for the porch swing still embedded in the ceiling. I could hear the creak of the swing, although it was no longer there. Inside, I sensed the presence of the elderly couple who had only recently departed. I pictured them, sweet-faced, living there quietly with the musty smell of unaired rooms and faded

dust-filled carpets, sitting lightly on antique chairs, listening to an heirloom clock chime the hours. Ghosts.

I told Herm what I was thinking.

"Yes," he said, "but they would not be sitting on antique chairs. I remember very well the kind of furniture they had in these bungalows. Much more likely to be one of those bulbous sofas."

I changed the image in my mind, although I liked the idea of delicate antique chairs. Perched on the bulbous sofa, which was upholstered in carved taupe plush, the old lady's feet did not even reach the floor, she was so small.

The agent showing the place was a business-like young man in sharp clothing. He obviously did not consider the bungalow fit for human habitation, but pointed out that it might be a good investment, as the business section of the city was expanding in this direction. Rezoning was sure to come, the land would be valuable.

"What a pity," I said.

5. Every house has its special aura. The last one on our list had an aura of malevolence. It looked quite ordinary, in a style known as Builder's Nondescript. But hostility oozed from the walls, crept up and down the stairs. It sent out vibrations of darkness and danger.

What caused this? Perhaps the basic nature of

the builder himself, or one of his subcontractors —a disturbed plumber, a star-crossed plasterer; perhaps the spirit of the land on which the house stood, or the shades of displaced dryads whose trees were felled by the bulldozer.

Herm tapped the bathtub to see if it was cast iron or only steel. It is something he does routinely with enameled tubs, to determine the quality of the building. It is his opinion that a steel tub indicates cheap construction throughout.

I tugged at his arm. "Let's go, Herm. This place is spooky."

We turned away from the house to face a sunset flaunting the high school colors, orange and blue.

"Rain tonight," Herm predicted.

It had been a thoroughly satisfying afternoon, and now how lovely it was to come home, to a place that was neither a palace nor a shanty but just a smart little house, its windows reflecting, from the western sky, a final blaze that splashed all over and illumined it as if in alpenglow. Herm did not seem to notice and I did not mention it. How could I admit that the Pink House had been found? Surely that would be the end of our Snoopnose excursions. I felt unutterably sad.

I went in and stood at the window. Herm joined me and put his arm around my shoulders.

"It's all right, Sugar," he said. "We'll pretend we haven't found it yet."

"You knew it all the time, didn't you, Herm?" I said, tears running down my face.

" 'He that seeketh, findeth.' Matthew, chapter seven," he said. "Stop crying."

We stood there together looking at the darkening ocean and the city lights. Love grows, not gradually, as some say, but in spurts, in bursts of understanding, in moments of delight.

About the Author

Doris Read was born in New York City and received a degree in mathematics from Barnard College. Although she started writing at age eight (an uncompleted romantic novel), her first published piece was in the *Barnard Bulletin*, which assigned her to interview a prominent Nazi sympathizer in his New York office shortly before World War II. He started by shouting "Hitler is the greatest man in the world!", which she used as the lead to her piece. After graduation she became a closet writer until 1977, when "Geranium," a love story about her car, appeared in *Small World*, the Volkswagen magazine. Since then her short stories have been published in *North American Review*, *Kansas Quarterly*, *Wind*, and other literary magazines.

Doris Read lives and writes in California.